# Curse Bound

## Imogene Nix

# INTRODUCTION

Curse Bound is one of those stories that took a long time to write. About 4 years from the inception and it feels like it's been stealing gold from a dragon! There've been some patient people waiting - Peta, that includes you! (Peta won the chance to be in the book at a Rotary function years ago. At that point, I didn't envisage just how long this book would take to be finished!)

So, in no particular order let me thank:

Keri for coining the book title - Curse Bound. Great title.
Suzi, Sassie, Keri (my "tribe" who always have my back.)

Imogene Nix's Makers & Fakers - you guys are fun! Thanks for being interactive and involved readers and giving feedback.

To Mr Nix, and the two baby Nix's... I finally did it. It's here! Written. Finished. Eu-flopping-reka! I did doubt myself at times but we're finally there.

To my wonderful editor - the always luscious "S" and to Jessica from Sinfully Sweet Designs for the cover.

As always, thanks to you too, readers. That's why I keep going. One book at a time. One story at a time. Thank you for joining me on this journey.

Imogene

2021

Print ISBN 978-1-922369-13-0

Imogene Nix ® is a Registered Trademark

# Why not subscribe to

# Imogene Nix's newsletter?

## PROLOGUE

*I couldn't possibly guess how much could change when I returned to my childhood home on the Island.*

# CHAPTER 1

*y dearest Tabs.*

*How I wish I wasn't writing this letter. I'd far rather have been there, by your side, when you go home. For home it is. The best home we've ever known.*

*There is so much to tell you, and yet, how do I even begin?*

*My sweet daughter, you lit my life from the moment you were laid in my arms.*

*Everything you did caused me unending delight and pleasure. I don't want to say goodbye, but the doctors have told me honestly, my time is short.*

*I need to tell you so much!*

*Our family has a long and proud history of sight...*

stared at the missive. Strangely, it all made sense, while memories long buried in my psyche rose up. Images of my mother, sick with her fingers curled and a look in her eye which frightened me as a child. I gave a tiny shake even now, remembering her eyes. I glanced back down to the paper splotched with salty water that dribbled and dripped. Another tear fell to join those on the lined paper.

I dropped it to the wooden tabletop and sat, numb.

At twenty-three, I was alone.

My hand curled around the glass of wine, and I dashed the tears from my face.

"I'd rather you were here, Daddy. I'd rather you guided me and not left some stupid bit of paper telling me I have to complete some stupid family quest!" I ended on a scream, then dropped my head to the tabletop. "Not even midday and you're talking to yourself. Great start to the next part of your life, Tabs."

*There is one task though, something I urge you to take seriously lest you never find your own deep and abiding love. The one I never found. As was the case for my mother and my grandfather. Neither was happy with their choice of partners.*

Suddenly, I didn't want the wine. I didn't want the silence of this house. I shoved from the table; the chair overturning and I whirled, ready to hurry from the house when something—someone—stopped me in my tracks. "Who the...?" I couldn't believe the sight before me.

A sad woman, pale and transparent, pinned me with her eyes.

It felt surreal, like I'd walked into some kind of weird television series. "Who are you?" I demanded, the entire time wondering what the hell was going on. Was I hallucinating?

*"Michael is lost, as am I. We need you. Only with your assistance can we be free."*

I glanced around looking to see if there was some kind of projection, sure at any second, someone would dive out and screech, "You've been punked." I even tried waving my hand through the hologram, but I slid through the image. Nothing shone, and I shivered.

"Are you a ghost?" I felt downright stupid for my comment. My stomach plummeted as the air around me seemed to freeze. "Who are you and what do you want?"

A sad smile flitted over the — and here I hesitated to consider the word — "ghost's" face.

*"I am Alice and you must find the Captain. My love, Michael."*

The frozen cube of ice that was presently my belly wobbled. "I wouldn't know where to start."

*"Finding Michael is the key. Find him and give us both peace."* She raised a hand and seemed to fade before my gaze.

"Wait!"

She smiled sadly. *"There isn't much I can tell you, except beware those who will drag you from the path. There are those who will tempt and lie. The very demons of hell."*

"Demons?" I scoffed, and she brushed her hand across her sad eyes.

*"You don't remember yet, and this too will dull in your memory, but soon. Someone will come and they will help you see clearly."* Then she wavered from view and disappeared.

I shook my head. "No," I told myself and hunted the corners of the room, but the reality slammed hard into me. "I've just had a conversation with a ghost. One who needs my help. Either I need medical care, or I need to find the answers."

# CHAPTER 2

*B*ags were packed haphazardly into my car, and I was backing away all within an hour. I knew the ferry was due by mid-afternoon and it would take time to navigate my way back to the main track.

In my head, whirling plans were forming.

Even as I'd rushed out the door I looked back, sure I feel a wrenching sadness as I retreated, but for the first time, I was safe in the knowledge I'd soon return to this place, if only to learn more about the tale my father had woven into his last letter to me.

"I'll be back as soon as I can. I need to arrange a few things first." I laughed. I'd just spoken to the house as if it were a sentient being. For all my foolishness, though, I planned to be back here within a week or two. First, I needed to sort out some leave.

"*T*abitha, I'm not sure I can give you three months' leave on such short notice. I can probably manage a week or two here and there."

I shook my head, looking at Donald and wondering what I'd ever seen in him. Today he looked distinctly harrowed, with his blond hair sticking up in haphazard spikes. His face carried the bloaty puffiness of someone who lived far too well, and his blue eyes that I'd once likened to a sparkling powder blue just looked icy.

"Donald, I've got over six months' worth of leave built up. I've never taken any other time off except for when Dad died and the occasional weekend. If you won't grant my leave, then I'll resign and take the lot in one lump sum. It's really your choice."

He winced. "But I can't afford it right now. You handle the staff and—"

I cut off his whine with a slashing hand gesture. "Your choice, but I'm going away, whatever you decide. So make it quick."

"Dammit Tabs, don't push me around otherwise I'll take your resignation."

"Fine. Done. Pay me out and I'm gone." I didn't feel a scrap of remorse. I'd already put the house on the market and Lana, the agent, felt sure it would be a quick sale.

I marched to the office, started shoving my stuff into the material shopping bags I'd brought with quick jerks. I felt light and as if I'd made the right decision. Once I got home, I'd be ringing the lighthouse administrators and making my formal request to move there indefinitely. I couldn't quite believe how easy it was.

"Look, Tabs—" Donald followed me to the office and stood like a gate in the doorway.

"No, Donald. I've got responsibilities. Things I have to do and I need time. You won't give me what I need so I'll just..." I waved my hands in the air and I could almost feel the seething fury that raced through him. "I have given you everything you asked for and more. I've filled in when you haven't had staff. I've run your kitchen, done taxes and everything in between. It's time you understood I'm an employee, not your slave."

He gaped fishlike at my last comment. Maybe it was a bit far-fetched, but still. He'd shown no consideration for my needs.

Finally, with the last item stashed, I scooped up my bags and pushed past him. "Send my paperwork to the PO Box, I've already got the house of the market." He goggled, and I smiled. "Goodbye Donald." Surprisingly enough, those words thrilled me.

I stepped out into the bright sunshine.

# CHAPTER 3

*E*xcitement built as I nosed my car through the long grassy driveway. The trailer I had attached to the back of my car carried all my worldly possessions. Well, the ones I'd chosen to bring with me. The rest—and I hadn't kept a lot—I'd stashed in a pay by the week storage facility on the outskirts of the town where I'd lived.

I'd ordered fuel to be delivered to run the generator I'd insisted be installed, so I had power for the important things, like the fridge I'd replaced and the oven. Lights weren't such an issue. The lamplight was sufficient for my needs, but I'd need it for the new computer and mobile telephone unit I'd invested in.

Now I was back, I had a mission. But my first stop was to get to the house, drop off everything I could, then head into town to collect my grocery order.

I couldn't wait to begin, but I needed to be methodical in my planning.

It had taken some time to find an archaeologist who specialized in marine research. Particularly in this region of the world. I'd been even more surprised to learn his name: Christian Monteith.

*Alice had been a Monteith before she'd married Michael.* Not for the first time, I wondered if there was a connection. Just as I had every other time I thought about my weird heritage, I scoffed at my fanciful thoughts. "Come on, Tabs. You need accurate data, not daydreams and ifs, buts or maybes!"

I stopped the car and gazed at my home. With my old house on the mainland sold, that's what this place was now. Home.

"No time like the present." I cracked the door open and stretched. It had been a long day, starting well before dawn, but I'd wanted to get going, start early and catch the first ferry.

I manhandled the cases one by one, the boxes of photographs and books. Then I started on the trailer. The mower and rakes, buckets and cleaning equipment. I'd left my bike in storage but included my father's equipment, which carried with it memories of time spent with him. Today, though, touching the rod made me wish I'd taken the time to fish with him, so I could claim a more tangible connection with him and the equipment. I shrugged off the sobering thought, reminding myself I'd chosen this item because I'd promised myself I'd learn to fish.

For a moment I breathed deeply, the shackles of everyday life falling away along with the unnecessary detritus of my life.

The small village at the base of the single hill hadn't changed much in my mind. Small, paint peeling and unappealing from the outside. Inside the tiny shops were havens with weatherboard interior painted in cool and classic colors of pale green, white and soothing yellow. The only appreciable change was the payment system and the fact that the shop size seemed to have shrunk somewhat.

At the counter I waited with a smile while a sunburnt customer— likely a tourist—paid for their purchases, then advanced.

"Hi. I've got an order for Tabitha O'Shaughnessy."

The woman serving blinked, then gave a small nod. "You're the one who's staying at the lighthouse?"

My small nod seemed to inflame her interest.

"So, your Dad is here too?"

"Uh, no. He passed earlier this year." I was getting better at answering these kinds of queries, but it still hurt to acknowledge he wasn't with me any longer. The lump lodged in my throat took a bit to clear, but I stared at her, and after a tiny humph, I decided I needed to focus on the positive. I pinned the woman with my gaze. "Is everything ready with my order?"

"Oh yes, dear. It is. Just let me grab it."

She rushed away, the bulk of her body swaying back and forth under floral material. The sigh that escaped between my lips was short, more a chance to regroup and rebalance myself.

"You're Tabitha O'Shaughnessy?"

The gravelly voice behind me had every nerve in my body vibrating.

Spinning left me with a sense of unreality. Bright blue eyes and a mass of golden hair married with a bronzed skin greeted me. "I... Yes. And you are?"

"Christian Monteith." He shoved his hand between us and I took it, noting dimly the warmth and strength that he exuded. "I didn't expect to see you." That was a bit of an understatement of course in his words, but my mind felt thick, like molasses had invaded it.

"I didn't expect to arrive for a few more days, but the job I was doing ended early. Umm, I arrived on the ferry earlier, so if you like, I'll be free this afternoon. That is, if you want to begin immediately." My words rattled into silence, rocketing out with no real thought. The need to cringe rose, but I fought it off valiantly.

"Yeah. I can do that. How about I head up around three'ish?"

I nodded just as the woman returned, lugging a large cold box. "There's more here, dear, but if you just take it out to your car..."

"I'll do that for you, if you tell me which one you drive?" Christian reached out, and the woman handed the box over. Now I was committed, but still unsure if I wanted things to happen this way. So soon.

I blinked owlishly then grimaced, realizing how dumb my thoughts were. I was contracting him to help me find remains, not embarking on a lifetime of sex and discovery. "It's the white Honda. But, it's full of stuff, and I need to rearrange everything."

"Not a problem. I'm free to help."

There was a commanding air about him that didn't quite rub me up the wrong way, but left me feeling wary and out of my depth. Raw.

An anxious moment or two passed before I gave a nod. "Okay."

I turned back to the counter, took delivery of the next box, and paid my bill. The cheery smile of the cashier made little impact though, as my mind spun thinking of the tanned man waiting outside by my car. He was imposing and altogether too much of, well, *man*. That was it. That's why I felt my equilibrium was being compromised. Problem solved, I told myself as I hefted the box and headed for the door. I'd been without a male partner for a long time and needed to scratch an itch.

He must have seen me hovering by the door, as he was there, in a flash, opening it wide. It was a curiously old world action that filled me with a burst of warmth.

"Thanks."

His broad grin stole my breath and left me reeling. *Get a grip, Tabs.* The pep talk to myself didn't work. The way the curl of heat coiled in my belly reminded me I was very much intrigued by this man. No way would I admit just yet to being *attracted*.

I shuffled the boxes and bags on the backseat, and he shoved the two large boxes in. "Do you need help when you get to your cabin?"

"Cabin?" I straightened and promptly thwacked my head. "Ouch!"

"Are you okay?"

Rubbing my head didn't really help, but I did it on reflex. "Yeah. Thanks."

"Are you okay to drive?"

"Oh yes. It's not far."

"But the campgrounds..."

Realization filtered through me. He thought I was staying in one of the tourist cabins. A broad grin spread over my face. The stretching of skin and muscles unused felt odd. "No. I'm staying at the lighthouse keepers house."

"Really?" Now his eyes flashed with excitement.

"Yes. My family owns the property and I'm staying there."

"I'm looking forward to seeing it. It's up the center track and off to the northern side of the island, isn't it?"

"Yes."

"I've only ever seen it from the outside. Is there any chance of a tour of the lighthouse itself?"

I shook my head. "No. I've not yet received the okay to do that. But if you like, when and if I do—"

"I'd love to," he enthused.

A tinkle of laughter escaped me. "Great. Okay, look, I better get up to the house and get this unloaded. I'll see you this afternoon." I stepped back, needing some space before the feeling, that sense of connection and interest, grew larger.

He gave a nod, and I swung open the car door and climbed within. The engine responded to the turn of the key and I pulled away, but even then, I couldn't stop myself from a final glance in the rear-view mirror.

Finally everything in the car was unpacked, though not quite put away. Gazing around my new domain filled me with a sense of excitement, energy and fulfillment. I'd never felt so damned great about where I lived or had the sense of purpose that now suffused every atom of my body. *This is where I'm meant to be.*

Expanding my lungs with the fresh sea air, I let the peace of the vista suffuse me. I surprised myself, realizing I didn't feel lonely. It was as if the captain and his lady and all those who'd come since loitered just beyond my vision, willing me to take this step.

"I will find you." The promise slipped from between my lips, but I didn't care. I needed them to know, understand, that I wouldn't give up until it was done.

I hauled up the suitcase and tugged it down the hall to my

bedroom. Even as I lay it on the bed, it was as if others watched over me.

"If I don't get this put away now, he'll be here and I'll have my hands full of clothing."

I shoved my hand deep into the side and dragged out the shoes I'd stuffed in there. Dropping them to the floor, I heard the thud and smiled. Before I could turn away, I got the distinct impression of being urged to put them in the small closet. "Don't like me being untidy, huh? I was meaning to do them once I had everything else done, but okay, if you insist."

I leaned down and picked up the sneakers and boots, but a piece of something, lay under the bed and caught my eye. "What's that?"

I kneeled down and scooted under the high metal edge of the bed. Blobs of dust and the remains of many years of grime had no doubt hidden this until now. I slithered under the bed far enough to run my fingertips over the jagged edge.

It was old. The paper thick and ridged, unlike anything I'd seen before. "Now what are you showing me?" The murmur was to those no doubt watching my hunt. It was funny how quick I'd adapted and accepted my new reality.

The board rose slightly with the next tug, the jagged edges scoring the paper before it slipped free and I tumbled down with the treasure in my grasp.

Shimmying out was harder, but I felt both an urgency and excitement flare.

I huddled on the floor beside the bed and gazed down, running my finger over the script, aged and darkened. The hazing of the parchments turning it almost the same brown as the floorboards.

I could barely make out the words. The dark script faded. Perhaps it was *Maranoa* or *Mariner*. I bit my lip, scrutinizing the text, wishing I knew the answer.

On a sigh, I cradled it and slumped back, using the wall to brace against. "If you're trying to tell me something, it would be easier if I could actually read it." A glow of temper edged my words, then with a sigh I rose. "I'll show this to Christian. He might have more of an idea."

Even as I brushed the dust from my clothing, the knocking of a fist on wood echoed through the cottage. "Speak of the devil."

I pushed away from the room and headed to meet my guest.

*N*ursing a coffee, I searched the face of the man sitting opposite me at the table. I'd told him everything I knew —well, almost everything. I couldn't exactly tell him about the ghostly dreams or the sensation that someone was watching me and shoving me to find possible clues.

I was reminded of what my father wrote in his last letter to me.

*We see what others cannot, but sometimes that places a heavy burden on us. Remember when you knew Mrs. Elditch was sick? You hounded her to see the doctor. Terminal cancer. No one else picked it up until you made her go. Old Betty swore until she died that you warned her about her car brakes. They found they'd corroded when she sold it. If not for you, she could have died. What you have... What we both had is special. A gift. One I could never explain to your mother.*

"This paper is quite old, but could be nothing. I mean, after so many people living in this house..." He raised a shoulder in some essentially Gallic attitude. He reached over and held out his hand. "Let me make a note of the information and grab a quick image. Then I might be able to check it against known scripts." He tapped away quickly at the notebook computer, then snapped a photo with his phone. "Great thing having all this technology at hand."

I nodded.

"So, okay, your family owned the cottage for all this time, gifted to the government on the understanding that family members can inhabit at will."

"I know it's unusual, but according to family lore, it was payment for services rendered to the government. Something covert, according to my father."

He smiled. "That's what they all say."

I wasn't sure if I should feel affronted or amused at his comment. Instead, I swiped another quick sip of my coffee and allowed my mind to weigh everything he'd imparted so far.

In my hand, I held a quick printout of the family tree. There on the second line from the bottom, several times removed, was his name: Christian Monteith. While at the bottom lay mine.

My initial thoughts had been proven correct, and it made me even more unsettled. I'd had a personal interest—if I was totally honest, I'd been somewhat interested in him. Now, learning we were *related* made it feel wrong.

"Whatever happened to the captain, he never made it home and his wife stayed here. She never married again and her son had no children, so there was no direct line. No one to chase down what happened to him. It feels wrong, Christian. I mean, that there's no record of his death..."

"I know exactly what you mean. In my family, it's almost a challenge, to find him. This time, you and I have technology, access to family records. There's so much more information at hand. And with the *Silent Girl*, and my sonar equipment, I'm sure we will find him."

I bit my lip, the urge to reach out and grab his hand overwhelming me. "So, where do we start?"

"This is going to sound ridiculous, but has anyone checked the crawl space between the ceiling and roof?"

"I don't know. I mean, I don't remember Dad ever going up there. The electrics only came at the end of the 70's and were done through the floor. The same with the gas."

"Then, I think that's as good a place to start. Do you have a ladder?"

I shook my head. "I didn't bring one, but I'm not altogether sure what's in the shed. We could check."

Together we rose and headed for the back door, the door swinging open before we reached it. I had a feeling it was the ghosts encouraging us again.

"They really want you to answer the question, don't they?"

"Who?" My voice wobbled slightly as I made out I didn't have a clue who—or what—he meant. After all, if he *was* inclined to believe in the ghosts, he would need to fess up before I did. I had no intentions of making myself look idiotic.

"Your ghosts."

I bit my lip, wondering if I could get away with playing dumb for a little longer, at least until I knew where he stood. "I don't..."

"Oh, come on, Tabitha. I know about them. Everyone connected to the puzzle does. They've haunted me for years, and I hoped that you and I together might finally find the answer."

When I turned, I knew he was earnest. The lump wedged in my belly shifted just a little. Maybe I wouldn't look so odd. "Okay, so the ghosts exist." I waited for the snicker, but none came. Satisfied, I nodded and continued, "At least as far as you're concerned. And me. But if I ever told anyone—"

"They'd laugh at us and maybe even suggest a psychiatrist. I agree. But I know, and so do you, that they're real. So, let's stop messing around and get on with the task they've set us."

"I guess I wondered why you'd taken this on. I'm asking for help to find a sunken ship without treasure. I didn't even get into the long-lost ancestor thing."

"Really, I accepted because it intrigued me. I haven't ever come across records of a ship, but you were so... adamant."

We stepped into the green backyard; the scents surrounding us both. At the shed, he reached out, his arm brushing my shoulder, and a frisson of excitement rippled through me.

I cleared my throat and the look he gave me warmed me to my bones.

"You think there's one in there?" He nodded at the rickety door and I shrugged.

"I don't have a clue, but if there is one, that's where we'll find it."

The door opened slowly, squeaking and protesting years of disuse.

Peering within showed darkness, interspersed with shadows and festooning cobwebs. My belly jiggled. "Uh, I think we're going to need a flashlight."

He snickered and reached into one of the deep pockets that decorated his three quarter khaki pants.

"Here." He drew out a pen like item, depressed a switch and light pierced the gloom.

"Okay."

"I was a boy scout, back in the day."

A chortle broke free. "Back in the day? You aren't exactly old you know."

He winked. "No, but it's a great pick up line."

I didn't have an answer for that one, so decided silence was probably the right course of action.

He stepped inside the shed, slowly casting the illumination left and right. With each step I crowded behind him, unwilling to be left behind but wary of the what could be in here.

A step to the left, advance a few more steps, skirt around some bulky mass. "Ah! Just what I figured." He moved swiftly now, and I stepped behind him, then onto something long and thin.

"Ah!" My heart thudded painfully in my chest while beads of cold sweat broke over my brow and body.

He flashed around, "what?"

"A snake?" I barely whispered, and he turned the glow in the direction of my feet.

"Just a hose." He reached out, hand sliding over my shoulder, and I steadied.

For a moment it was calm and peaceful and I swear, I could have been lost in his touch, then reality intruded. I'd clearly been away too long.

"Okay now?" He spoke softly, breaking the spell he placed over me, and when I nodded, he turned away and grabbed the old ladder.

Step by step we retreated, clattering and thumping as the wooden rails and posts banged against the contents of the building.

It was only when we reached the safety of the outside that I noted the layers of dust and threads of old cobweb that I realized how dirty we had become. Even as I reached for him, to dust away the mess that I felt the creep at my collar.

"OhMyGod!" I flicked ineffectually at it, and he brushed away the spider.

"Okay now?" He repeated the words, a gleam of amusement in his gaze.

"I sound like an idiot."

"Not at all." His assurance made me feel downright silly. "Arachnophobia is common enough that I don't think it's silly. Now, we should get inside and see what I can find in the crawlspace."

*H*e clambered back down, while I steadied the ladder, an awkward shuffle as he dragged something small with him. *A chest? Would it all be that simple?*

Christian grunted a little as he hefted the weight and it dropped to the top run of the ladder.

"You can pass it down to me."

Without moving his feet, he grabbed both sides and bent. The ladder wobbled, and I grabbed hold, steadying it.

"Not sure this is the best way."

I agreed, but either he'd have to climb down, his hands steadying it—not the best choice, I thought—or it would fall.

Bracing the ladder with my shoulders, I reached up. "Pass it now."

This time, though the ladder shuddered, he managed to get it into my hands. I gave an *oomph*. It was heavier than I expected. He stayed still while I put the old wood on the floor and reached back. Then he climbed slowly down, replacing the board.

At the bottom, he slumped. "I could sure use a water. It's dusty and hot up there." It must have been, because rivulets of sweat marred the gray of his t-shirt and his hair was plastered against his skin.

I allowed myself just a moment to bask in the pleasure of the find, running my fingertips over the casket. The metal was ridged, as if the cobwebs and who knew what else had adhered themselves to the surface. Excitement bubbled inside me. *Was this the answer?*

I turned, opened the cupboard, ran the faucet and finally returned to Christian, a glass of cold clear water in my hands and passed it to him, waiting anxiously as he drank it down. "What else is up there?"

"Some boxes with clothing, but they're reasonably new, I'm guessing from around fifties and sixties. A box of toys and another of old bolts of material. I can grab that later for you, if you'd like. In the back corner, there was another box, which had what looked like old photos. I couldn't reach it easily, and think it might be a fair bit heavier than this. Oh and a tea chest. One of those old square ones."

I bit my lip, wondering what that might contain. It amazed me that these old things belonging to my family had remained here. I'd have thought the government would have cleared them out when they took possession of the property. Or leased it... or however they described assuming their use of the property, even though we still stayed as owners. Clearly I'd thought wrong.

He indicated the chest at his side. "I'll bring a better ladder next time. Not sure this one would carry the combined weight."

I bit my lip, twin concerns for him and the contents of the mystery box weighing heavily on me.

"No. You're right. This one is dangerous, and I don't want you to get hurt. Besides, the photos have waited this long, they'll wait another day or two."

"So, how do we get into this box?" He gazed at me and I kneeled to inspect the latch.

"We need a key and I'm not keen on destroying the box to get it open. But if there's a key, where would it be hidden?"

I scratched at my head and felt the tangle of web in it. "Ugh! I need a shower."

Christian laughed. "So do I." A glance at his watch had him muttering. "Damn! Look at the time. I'm due at the school to pick up my Kira."

That blasted the wind from my sails. *Daughter? He was married?*

"I'm so sorry, Christian. I didn't realize." I bit my lip and inched away, furious with myself at my interest in a married man. "Do you need to call your wife?" I winced.

*Way to go Tabs. Fishing for information, which he hasn't offered.*

"My wife? Oh, you mean Kira's mother. We're divorced. I've got custody of Kira because Janet was more interested in city lights and parties than kids and school activities."

His words were an echo of my father's description of my mother.

*Your mother—she's hard to explain to you. You are still so young, and life is black and white. If only all life was that simple.*

*It's vital you remember, above all, your mother was both a mistake and the best choice of my life. She didn't love me. Bringing her to the island was something she could never forgive me for.*

*I was always left with the pondering thought that maybe she was there for a reason, her interest in me and the house indicative of something. Yet I never questioned it further, as it was both my destiny and my heritage.*

*For all her faults, she gave me you. My beautiful daughter.*

*I have never harbored any hard feelings towards her because of that. In that short time we were together, she gifted me with the most marvelous thing of all.*

Funny, how two men, lightly related, could experience similar relationships. I became aware that he was watching me, and I'd not responded. Was this some kind of weird magical shit I was doomed to follow if we didn't complete this quest?

How the hell did you say 'her bad luck,' without looking somehow needy and interested? "I'm sorry."

"Don't be. Kira's happy and well-adjusted and it happened a couple of years ago."

"Your daughter, Kira? How old is she?"

"Ten. Kira's a smart kid. Tops her class, mostly. Wants to be an oceanographer when she leaves home. Thinks what I do as a maritime historian and archaeologist is interesting, but she'd rather be in the water poking around, while I prefer the bookish side of things. "

I gawped. "Bookish side? But you've got all kinds of equipment and your boat—"

"I don't mind getting wet when I'm interested, but it's the history that grabs my attention. Like Michael. He's intriguing, the way he disappeared. The stories that were told about him, you know, how he did things and this was his repayment. That intrigues the hell out of me."

I knew exactly what he meant as I rose. Christian did too. "I have to go, but tomorrow, I can swing by, say around nine? Then we can look at the chest." He peered close. "You will wait for me, won't you?"

I nodded. "I don't want to damage anything and you're the history geek, so I'm more than happy to wait."

Apparently satisfied, he gave a curt nod. "Good. Tomorrow at nine."

He'd be back, so why did I feel this damned wrench as he left. Instead of focusing on the way I felt?

I snapped the ladder open, yowling when one leg cracked and crashed down on me. "Serves me right." I gathered up the remains, my hand stinging, and dumped it outside the door.

"Maybe next time, don't let it break on me," I informed the ghosts of the cottage and swept out of the room determined to shower.

# CHAPTER 4

*C*rawling into bed, I was a little frustrated at my inability to find the key to the chest. I'd promised Christian I wouldn't open it without him, and I wouldn't. But if I could find the key, then we'd be able to open it without damaging the wood, which seemed important to me. So I'd hunted high and low, through every cupboard, behind every door and in each drawer, but it remained missing.

I dragged the sheet up over my body. "Night everyone."

Sleep came quickly, stealing my senses until I floated away.

*"You're here." This time, instead of a dream, the Captain, my ancestor Michael, extended his hands. "Never before have we been able to connect like this."*

*Where was I that I'd come face to face with this man? I could detect nothing beyond him, and all around was wispy vapor, as if a cloud surrounded me. The white of my surroundings cloyed.*

*The skin of his palm rasped over mine, calluses sliding against my softer flesh, dragging my gaze back to his. I could feel him. Wherever we were, we were both, at the same time, corporeal to each other. Shock and fear raced my heart.*

*"What?" I shook with trepidation, wondering what my dreams had led me into.*

*"This is no dream, girl. You are here, in the other place, with me. You've accepted the task of freeing me and my beloved from this endless torture."*

*"This can't be real. I mean, I believe in ghosts, but they're not... you know. I can't touch them."*

*His laugh boomed while the blue eyes crinkled. "Not normally, but here, in this place, I'm no ghost and neither are you what you would be awake. This is the place between life and death. Some may call this purgatory." His jacket rose and fell as he shrugged.*

*"But I'm not dead. Why am I here?"*

*"I have no words to explain, only that I have existed here, without my beloved for a long time. Years, decades, and I think more than a century. I seek peace and a way back to my Alice." I detected exhaustion and sadness in his words. They tugged at my emotions.*

*"I want to help you. I will help. But where do we begin when I can't even find the key to the damned chest? I'm sure it's where we should start."*

*"I know nothing of the journey you must take, only that Alice had a chest. It was where she kept things of importance before our marriage and since. She kept the key about her person, on a long chain."*

*I bit my lip, wondering which chain. I'd seen one long ago. My father had shown it to me once and said he kept it among his photos. It seemed too easy that it would be the first one I'd remember.*

*I tried harder, recalling what I'd seen. Another looked more like a belt and hung in what had been my mother's room, and a third reminded me of a necklace. It was in the jewelry collection my father had gifted me when I'd turned eighteen. Each were adorned with keys and various items. The one my father had kept had been in a box. I wasn't even sure it was one I'd brought with me? Tomorrow I would check. If it wasn't there, then I'd need to make a trip to the mainland.*

*"I cannot stay with you here." His words echoed. I glanced up, shocked that he seemed less substantial. So many questions crowded my mind.*

*"Did she keep a diary? Did you? What else do I need to know?"*

*His fading smile turned sad. "If I could tell you more, I would. But the answers are not mine to give. You must seek the truth yourself. For that is the way that leads to what you need to know."*

*Light blurred around us, and vertigo slashed through me. His gaze widened as I pressed my hand to my quivering belly. "I must leave you now. Whenever you need me though, I will be here." The words echoed as the Captain disappeared from sight.*

*S*tarting awake, my heart thumping rapidly beneath my breastbone, and stark fingers of lightning illuminated the night sky. "Oh my God!" My stomach settled, the roiling sickness that coated my throat abating, leaving a gaggy burning sensation.

A crash shattered the solitude, and I rose, fumbling out of the bed. Cold wind whipped around my feet as I hunted for the slippers.

The light nightgown I'd slipped over my body offered very little warmth as my limbs chilled in the pre-dawn, storm-lashed cold air. I groped for the wardrobe door as another flash cracked close to the house.

I'd always loved storms, but there was a sense of something more about this one. *Was it because of my dreamlike encounter with the Captain or my own tightly drawn nerves?*

On gaining the lounge, I could see what had caused the crash and the cold air. The latch on a window had torn free and the shutters I'd neglected to close gaped open. I fought the dragging wind and driving rain, my feet slipping for purchase on the soaked wooden floors until I finally closed the opening.

Shivers wracked my body, and I might as well have been totally naked, as the nightgown plastered itself to my body.

"Better shower and change, Tabs." A swift glance at the clock on the mantle assured me dawn, if it broke through the storm would come soon.

Stepping beneath the warm spray of water, I let the sensations flood my body, beating back the cold that had chilled my core. "I wonder how Christian is getting on." It occurred to me I didn't even know where he lived on the island. The tourist accommodation didn't seem likely. There were workers' cottages on the far side, nearest the ferry for those employed by the state government and of course, some long-term residents had houses dotted in the wilderness here and there.

"Possibly near the ferry where the boats are moored." I gave a nod. But just that thought of Christian had the memory of his form, the way his eyes crinkled in the corner... Well, now that got things warming up, I thought with a little grin.

"Hmm, Tabs. Too long and no man means you wish for something you can't have at inappropriate times. You're here to solve the problem and get your life sorted. That means the man drought continues." I let my words die away on a sigh. I knew all that, but he was good looking, interesting and... I shrugged.

Instead, I dressed quickly and set about cleaning up the mess from the storm which had died away leaving the area smelling fresh, scents of greenery floated on the air, though it still seemed rather dull. I knew the clouds would soon melt away and the heat of the day would banish my dreams.

"I should write down what happened."

So, after clearing away, I popped the kettle on the gas stove and waited for the whistle that told me the temperature was right, poured myself a steaming brew and settled at the kitchen table with my computer.

I tapped away everything I could remember, everything he'd said, then scanned my words. "Good thing this is a private computer, otherwise people would think I'm nuts."

Settling back on the wood seat, I closed my eyes, trying to remember which box I would have popped the photos into. The small one with pink writing came to me and I rose, reaching for scissors as I headed into my old room, where I'd dumped them all.

I pushed the other boxes out of my way and there it was, in the corner. With my fingers, I dug at the tape I'd used to hold the box closed and dragged the blade of the scissors across. It gave with a pop, the flaps springing up.

Bedding and toiletries were quickly tugged out and dumped on the unmade frame. I reached in, my fingers closing around the smaller box within, and I smiled. "Here they are."

Even as I hauled them out, I spied another box below. I couldn't contain my grin. My father's old transistor radio and his plug in CB unit. The chortle of delight filled the air. I liked the sound of my own company, but having some way to monitor the outside world had occurred to me when I'd packed, then I'd forgotten I'd stuffed them in there. And there was yet another link, one that filled me with warmth. Memories of hours spent hunched together, working on jigsaw puzzles by the radio or listening to the antics of truckers and other enthusiasts dotted my childhood.

"Thanks again, Dad." If only he was here for me to thank him in person. The slow slide of sadness edged along my heart, and an ache settled in my guts as I sighed. Time to put aside my grief again, I reminded myself.

I hauled my spoils to the kitchen, finding plugs for the items and sliding the box of photos back to the tabletop.

"So, what exactly is in here?" I had studiously avoided going through the box since my father's passing. It had seemed too big, *too much* at the time, so I'd stuffed everything into a box and stayed busy. Until now.

Sliding the lid back, the glow that I'd held tight frittered away, as the pall of grief settled again.

The first photo, the one on top, was the last one taken with my father at school. Me in a formal gown and he in his one suit. The one I'd asked for him to be cremated in. Tears welled, fat burning pools that trickled down my face. I caught sight of the old transistor radio in the background, sitting on the entertainment unit in the lounge room. I grinned and ran a shaking finger over the image. "I wish you were here, Dad. You'd know what to do."

On a sigh, I laid it aside and picked up another. There he was, reclining on wooden seats at the cricket. I remembered that day well. The wild sunburn I'd returned home with, that Dad had warned me against, had hurt for days. Of course, if only I'd listened and worn my hat.

Another was a school photo, me with knee-high socks and a buck-toothed grin. Each image reminded me of what we'd had together. The good times and the bad. The things that had hurt the most and the extreme highs.

I swiped away a droplet of saltwater as I came across the bundle of letters, tied with a green satin ribbon. I knew the handwriting. My mothers.

Thinking back to the letter he'd written me, the one I'd read on the day I'd said goodbye, I wondered if I was strong enough yet to read what she'd written. Possibly, I determined and laid them aside to consider later. At the bottom sat an old manila envelope, foxed and hazed with time. The script was scratchy but addressed to my father care of the island post office. The outline of something large within it drew my gaze and carefully I lifted it out, peered within and gasped. An old necklace, dotted with greenish stones. Two earrings, twin to the necklace and some kind of chain. The one I'd seen before. Dangling in among the tarnished silver scissors and bag was a key. The brass had turned green, but excitement buzzed through my veins.

Perhaps this is what I sought. I snatched up the item, then grimaced as it clanged. "Maybe I should be a little more careful," I reminded myself. It was, after all, an antique. It could also be the key to the chest. The link that I just *knew* would give us the next step.

In my excitement, I hurried to the chest where I'd left it on the floor of the sitting room. Dropping to my knees, I almost shoved it into the lock before I stilled. "I should call Christian."

I knew he wouldn't argue, he'd understand my excitement, but it felt like he should be here. Maybe he'd want photos to document what we found. "Do I need gloves? What if I damage something inside it, just shoving it open?" I rocked back onto my heels. "I should ring him, then wait for him to get here."

*What if it's not the right key?* I bit my lip. Should I check? I slid the metal implement into the hole and it fit. I felt the way it filled the space. Yes, this was the one.

*I could peek...* No. I wouldn't. I'd ring Christian. Have him join me, I decided telling myself firmly that an hour or two wasn't a lot to ask.

Dragging myself away felt like a wrench. Reaching for the phone, I wondered how I could tell him about the finding of the key, then shrugged. He already believed in ghosts, so surely this wouldn't be too much more of a stretch.

**CHAPTER 5**

Christian arrived promptly at nine o'clock. "You found it? You're sure it's the right key?" Excitement flowed from him, leaving the air buzzing.

"It sure is. In fact, I popped it in and..." the skin of my face flamed and I bit my lip.

He frowned just a little. "You opened it?"

The fluttering in my belly stopped as I shook my head. "Oh, no. I wasn't sure I should open it, just in case something got damaged. I just... I slid the key into the lock to check. Nothing more."

He smiled then. The generous curve of his lips had those darn butterflies doing backflips in my stomach.

"Excellent. I brought gloves for both of us, and I had some acid free parchment to lay the items within on, while we examine the contents."

Well, clearly Christian had experience with this kind of thing or thought of everything. I mentally kicked myself. Of course he had experience. He was a marine archaeologist.

"You've done this kind of thing before? Open old chests?"

He chortled. "Not quite like this, but yes. I've opened old stuff before."

"So I did the right thing by not opening it?" I encouraged him to follow me back to the kitchen where I'd sat the chest on a chair. Once there, I felt flustered. What the hell did I know about putting ghosts to rest and looking for remains? And how on earth had I managed to get such a good-looking man, like Christian, to visit me at home. I waved my hands around in the air for a moment, then decided I should really be busy. "Coffee?"

"Not right now. I'd prefer we didn't have anything near the casket when we open it." He softened his words with a tiny smile. But I still felt idiotic.

"You can take the photos for me, though. I'd really like to document every step."

He'd thrown me a lifeline, and I grabbed it, stepping closer. I could smell the subtle spiciness of his cologne now, and my mouth watered. Along with another part of my anatomy.

Christian extended the small digital camera. "It's a point and shoot, so you can't go wrong."

"Sure." Mentally, I fumed at myself. I wasn't that stupid. I knew what to do. So why was I letting my body get carried away?

"Ready?"

The single word cut through the cloud of insightfulness. "Yeah."

He extended his hands, turned the key. Nothing except a creak. "I think it's stuck. Hang on, I've got some machine oil in my box, but I'd rather not use it if I don't need to." He pulled the key free, peered inside. "Let's try one more time, to be sure." This time, he tried again and something gave. You could tell it still stuck, though, as if pushing against the tumbler before it turned swiftly. He swore but pulled away.

Ran his hand over his face and I realized he'd started sweating, as he'd been working the lock.

Click! I took a photo of the key in the lock. I didn't know exactly how much he wanted, but too much was better than not enough, I reasoned.

Now he reached out, tracing his fingers over the wood, as if search the memories by braille. "So, the first step. Be ready." His hand splayed out over the lid and I snapped photo after photo as he carefully levered the top back.

A mass of items, what looked like letters tied with a tattered ribbon, jewelry and knick knacks filled it up. "Oh!" Even as I whispered a puff of dust rose.

Another photo had the shutter making a clicking noise.

Christian tugged on the gloves and reached into the chest.

"Let's see what we have here..."

gazed in wonder at the collection that now adorned the table. In the time it had taken to carefully check, photograph and remove every item, my eyes had grown as wonder after wonder was revealed.

A tiny scrap of pale blue material, a hand knitted bonnet and a faded, crushed flower had been revealed when tissue paper was unfolded. Some items were easy to know the history of. Others left me wondering. Where had the flower come from? The long ago Michael or their child, Albert?

A pile of letters, each carefully tied with a ribbon and the broken seals, told of the connection between Michael and Alice. Many bore signs of water damage reminded me he'd been a captain at sea for long months at a time. Where had he written them and how had they reached her?

A long string of pearls was hidden with a tie pin. The golden masculine item was old and boldly designed, set with a single stone. I'd bet my last dollar that it was a ruby.

My heart thudded in my chest.

I imagined the pain Alice must have felt when the tiny bag they'd been stashed in had been knotted and placed in this chest for safe keeping. But why was it stashed in the roof cavity? Without an answer, I let my gaze wander further still.

A small miniature painting of Alice and her Captain was nestled with a small photo, hazed and brown. It showed a woman and a child. The woman shrouded in black, her veil pushed from her face as she stared steadily ahead. The child was little more than a babe. I knew that was her before I glanced at the tightly drawn features.

The last item, though, was the one I was sure would hold some answers. A leather-bound journal, the black cow hide faded and pitted. The spine creaking as I inspected it. I wondered how much of her soul she'd poured into it and sighed before returning to the photos. They alone told a story of loss and remembrance.

I pointed with a shaking finger to that photo. "It must have been hard for her."

"Times were tough for widows. That she never remarried showed she was strong and likely financially well placed."

I frowned. "Why do you say that?"

"Lots of women who lost their husbands remarried. They needed a breadwinner and a stable influence for their children. That she didn't and we don't know that she undertook work outside the home means that she had to have some means to provide for herself and her child."

I bit my lip, pondering his words. What kind of work could she have done? Washing? Most of the small townships I knew of had Chinese laundries. Perhaps taking in boarders? That didn't gell with a woman on a small island and a tiny child.

"What things could she have done? I mean, we don't know her educational background. It's a small island, and I doubt there would have been much in the way of lodging needed. So what?"

"Those are all good questions, Tabs. There could be an answer in the diary."

As if my hands had heard the comment before he'd made it, I'd already reached out to run a fingertip over the covering.

"You should be the one to open it." I heard the excitement in Christian's voice. I wanted to open it. I needed to know the answers, but fear of damaging the fragile pages held me back.

"I don't want to damage it."

"The covering is pitted and old, but its general condition is quite good. I wouldn't suggest photocopying pages or bending the spine hard, but it looks readable."

Carefully, and with a fair amount of trepidation, I opened the first page. The spine creaked slightly as if protesting the action, and I glanced back at Christian. He nodded and indicated I should read aloud.

*January Twelve, 1880*

*The Captain has once more left me and the house is devoid of his presence. The walls enclose me like an empty tomb, and I'm sure I'll perish from my grief. Three weeks is not nearly enough to celebrate his return, but I am thankful for what little time is mine with him. This voyage, he brought me gloves and a cape from Paris. Ribbons and lace from Ireland and a tiny carved comb from the Indies. It is made of bone and is delightful. Small yet delicate. I will keep it on my toilette table.*

*I fear this will be a long and difficult voyage for my love. The missive he received last Sunday night made his mouth flatten and eyes turn cold. He didn't reveal the contents to me, however I know my husband and his moods. Since then he has not settled. I fear the promise he made me, before we wed, that he'd refuse any more special tasks has come to naught. The Captain is a man of honor and if they've drawn him back into the world of spies, there is little I can do but hope.*

*The weather is most inclement and he will be sailing into the cold seas. I pray that is all he meets. The Captain assures me that on his return, that he will stay longer and perhaps undertake less lengthy journeys. For all his careful words, my mind runs to the many things that could turn wrong on this trip, and I fear for him greatly. Yet, I am a woman and a wife. My role is to wait for him, care for the house, and pray for his safe return.*

*Mrs. Grantly from the village is to return today...*

I skimmed the rest of the entry and sighed. "She's sad the Captain has left. The trip he was undertaking wasn't clearly defined, but wasn't trade. She worried that he'd remain safe and the weather he was sailing into would be difficult going. I got the impression there was something... not quite right, about the trip. She doesn't say what though."

Christian grunted from across the table as he watched me. "Anything else?"

"After that, it's about a Mrs. Grantly. Some recipes and general things. I get the impression this was before she knew she was pregnant even."

"That would make sense. Albert was born in late 1880, or so the story goes."

"Story?"

"Her sister, my direct line, stated in her journal that Alice was quite reclusive and only told them about Albert after he was born. There's some conjecture as to the actual date of birth."

"That's odd." Tabitha frowned, pondering over the information revealed. *Hiding. Not letting the family know till after the birth.* "There's no chance he was adopted?"

Christian stared at her. "Not that I know of... But it's also a great point. I mean, hiding away here, not seeing anyone much." He shook his head, a lock of blonde hair dropping forward. "No. I think Cynthia would have known." Clearly, though, he wasn't convinced, because his face was tighter than before.

"Could we maybe, you know, read from the diary? Perhaps there is a clue in there to what happened to Michael and when Albert was actually born?"

Christian glanced at his watch, "I need to go. Why don't you get started, make some notes, and when I drop by after the weekend, we can talk about it."

I bit my lip. I'd totally forgotten that it was a Friday. Maybe it was a quirk of living here. I honestly couldn't ever remember forgetting like this before.

"Yeah, sure."

He rose and held out his hand, and while I reached for it, I wasn't sure I was ready for the feel of his skin against mine. Not that I expected anything, I told myself. The shock that rippled through my nervous system left me with a mushed brain and tingling parts.

Even as he dragged his hand away, his eyes felt as if they bored into mine. Was he wondering about the connection between us? Maybe he didn't feel it and I was just a fool. Determined to put that behind me, I escorted him to the door. "Well, have a great weekend."

He stepped over the threshold, while I remained at the door, holding it open. "Look, what are you doing tomorrow? I'm taking my daughter fishing. Would you like to join us?"

Lost for words, I looked at him. A tinge of red crested his cheeks, and I realized he was *embarrassed.*

"I don't want to intrude."

"It's all good. Kira will enjoy someone else to talk to. Besides which, she's terribly interested in this place and hoping you'll invite her up some day."

A laugh escaped. "Well, when you put it like that, sure. I'd love to."

He grinned. "Then we'll pick you up around nine'ish?"

"Sounds good. What should I bring?"

He leaned in. "If you can cook...? Anything."

"Fine. Sweet? Savory?"

"Kira's not a sweet-thing kind of kid. But I could be talked into a sweet treat or two." He backed away and I watched as he turned.

My mind raced as I thought over the recipes I had the makings for. Maybe some mini quiches, savory muffins and even a cinnamon teacake. Simple and easy to transport.

I kept busy baking the goodies for the following day.

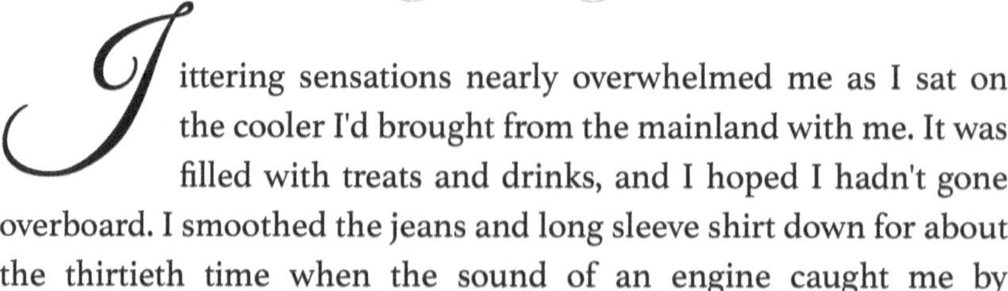

*J*ittering sensations nearly overwhelmed me as I sat on the cooler I'd brought from the mainland with me. It was filled with treats and drinks, and I hoped I hadn't gone overboard. I smoothed the jeans and long sleeve shirt down for about the thirtieth time when the sound of an engine caught me by surprise. Gripping my hat and oversized tote bag in my hand, I rose, cupping above my eyes to cut through the glare.

A mini moke wove its way up the track to stop outside my gate.

Christian smiled and climbed out of the car while inside a smaller and more feminine version of him looked on.

"Come on, pumpkin. Come meet Tabitha."

The girl joined her father; the door slamming behind her and Christian winced. "I'd like a door left on the car by the time you're old enough to drive it."

Kira grinned and rolled her eyes as if she'd heard that saying a million times. He ruffled her hair, then strode purposefully in my direction.

"All set?" He gazed at the cooler and back to me. "Wow, I hope you've got something homemade in there."

"Uh huh." I grinned, and he leered.

"Going to tell me?"

"Nope. You'll need to wait and see."

On a sigh, Christian hefted the cooler. "It's heavy. I'm sure we could lighten it..."

As I tugged on my bag, the weight shifted and I slid. I hadn't seen Kira enter the yard, but there she was, reaching out and offering support. Once I got myself sorted out, I smiled at the girl. "Thanks. You must be Kira?"

"Hi Ms. O'Shaughnessy."

Up close, I was amazed at how like her father she was. She shared her father's blonde hair and bright blue eyes, however unlike Christian, she was exceptionally tall for her age, gangly, but with the promise of a statuesque beauty.

"You right?" Christian's words reinforced how stupid I felt, and a burning blush covered my face.

"Yeah. It was one of those things." I sounded strangled, but Kira hovering beside me giggled.

"That's okay. Daddy and I do that kind of thing all the time."

The trip was short, down the road and a sharp turn left, then along a windy green-edged single lane. The twinkle of the water could be seen between the limbs.

The road suddenly turned, the trees cleared and unveiled a hidden gem, turquoise water lapping at the white rocks behind a secure compound met my gaze. "Where are we?"

"This is the private marina where we keep the Silent Girl." The boat ahead bobbed on the gently lapping waves at the end of a jetty of wood.

Another small vehicle was parked just beyond the chain-link fence and the flowing locks of another woman, tall and wrapped in skinny jeans, tank top and bright red boots.

A sharp pain lodged somewhere in my chest. Christian had brought another woman to our expedition and while my reaction shocked me, I had to accept it was because I wanted to capture his attention.

Christian stopped the car and climbed out, Kira flowed out of the back but I hung back, feeling unsure now.

"Come on, Tabitha! Grab the basket and we'll get the rest." The girls' chirp caught my attention, snapping me from the self-absorption I'd sunk into.

"Sure."

I hoisted the basket up and hung it over my arm, then pasted a smile on my face and followed Christian and Kira to the gate. It swung open with a loud squeak, Christian waiting for me to pass before releasing the spring-loaded door. The dull thud reverberating through my brain.

"Come meet my sister, Peta. She's going to be captaining today. Under direction, of course."

The icy knot inside my belly loosened. "Your sister?" I peered closely at the statuesque blonde, who grinned broadly.

"It's nice that Christian finally brought me a playmate. He's a bit shy, so there has to be something special about you." Peta extended her hand and I returned the shake.

"Well, I'm not sure about special, but I love boats. So this seemed too good an opportunity to pass up!"

Peta flashed a grin in my direction, then gracefully stepped over the side and onto the decking of the boat. I followed suit, the dip and sway of the boat reminding me of younger days in the rowboat with my father.

"Penny for your thoughts," whispered a voice behind me. *Christian.*

"I'm just thinking of my father."

He nodded. "I've heard of him. Sounds like he was a good man, staying on after your mother left."

"He was the best." I gazed out over the water, watching the swell and wondering what he'd think of my choices. I kind of thought he'd approve.

"You'd better get everything stowed away. I'd like to get moving!" Peta's words intruded and I moved with a jerk, nearly falling over the basket which I still held awkwardly in my hands.

Christian reached for it, his skin glanced mine and I smothered a gasp as a sharp flash of current ran between us.

With a tug, he pulled me in the direction of the cabin. Even after he'd headed back up to talk to his sister, I remained there, hiding out and trying to ignore the feelings he'd awoken in me.

## CHAPTER 6

*K*ira sat on the edge of the boat, dangling her feet while we all fed on sandwiches, fruit and the baked goods I'd brought along. The azure hue of the sea settled the nerves that jumbled and jumped in my belly while I waited for a tug on the line.

Not that there'd been a lot of biting. Or not from the fish.

"Come on, brother mine. You've never yet caught a fish bigger than me. Not ever." Kira chortled, and I listened in, wondering at the obvious affection between brother and sister.

What would it be like to have a sibling? I'd never really considered it. But then, I'd had my father and until his death, that had been enough for me.

The sun warmed our skin and imbued me with a sense of well-being.

The line jangled, a tiny bell on the end of the rod ringing imperiously. We all sat up, reaching for lines hoping it was ours.

Settling my hand to mine, I felt the insistent tug. "It's mine." I couldn't contain my breathless excitement.

Me. A first timer, catching a fish.

"Reel it in!" Kira slid in beside me, bouncing up and down, and I followed her instructions and Peta's. "Tug the line so it catches on the hook."

Wind. Wind. Wind. I tugged and wound and pulled a little more as the water rippled. Then the fish was there at the side of the boat. Christian reached over my shoulder, his arm around me, anchoring himself as he used the net. My body seized with excitement, every neuron dancing where our skin touched.

With an efficient movement, he scooped the red and silvery fish from the water and pulled it to the deck.

"Well done!" Peta's congratulations tangled with Kira's and I beamed, unable to prevent the moment pass without celebration.

"My first fish."

Christian turned and smiled. "And it's of legal size."

"What kind?"

"Snapper."

"We can eat it?"

The skin around his eyes crinkled at my question. "Well, yes we can. If someone else can catch one, then maybe it would be a great dinner for the four of us."

"Four? But you're planning on dropping me home when we get back to the jetty, aren't you?"

Peta's gaze zoomed to me. "You've just caught your first fish. That means celebration and someone cooking it for you. Unless, of course, you really want to eat alone."

The bubble of warmth grew a little bigger inside my chest as I looked at the three others gathered around me. "No. I'd love to share dinner with you." With that, the matter was decided.

The warmth of the kitchen extended beyond the latent heat of the day. Mugs sat on a cup tree, a bowl of fruit centered the kitchen table, an old round wooden affair, showing signs of wear but scrupulously clean. Photos and merit awards adorned the refrigerator, and an old copper kettle sat on the top of the gas range.

"It's lovely."

I ran my hand over the granite countertop while perched on a metal and leather stool. Kira had disappeared for a shower. Peta, on checking her phone as we drew into the harbor, had grinned and declared she had an offer of a hot date with the park ranger. Christian had commented wryly that being dumped for a hot bod with a killer smile smacked of abandonment, while Peta chuckled.

Her "You betcha!" had resulted in a shake of his head and shrug from Kira.

That just left the three of them to feed on six snapper, all caught by Christian, Kira and myself.

"Is there something I can do?" I felt extraneous, watching his confident handling of the fish.

"You can take care of the salad, if you like, or talk to me. I like a bit of company when I work." One hand lay flat against the scales as he filleted the fish. One fillet, then the other found its way into a bowl of flour.

Even as he reached for the second I slid off my chair and headed for the refrigerator. "Where would I find...?"

"Try the crisper drawer at the bottom. I've got lettuce, carrots, and tomato. Not sure what else."

Spying half a cucumber, pineapple and sultana's my brain whirred to life.

"I don't suppose you have some noodles or peanuts?"

He pinned me with his gaze.

"Why?"

"Well, I like a salad with a bit of you know..." I shrugged as a wide smile emerged.

"Sounds like a plan. Dressings are in the fridge too."

I rattled around, finding a large bowl, then washed, sliced and sprinkled. By the time I was done, he had slipped the fish into the freezer. "Give them a few minutes for the crumbing to set and we're ready."

I retreated to the stool and perched there as he poured me a white wine, which I gratefully accepted.

"So, your first fish."

"Yeah. Dad always tried to get me interested, but I decided it wasn't my thing when I was pretty young. I guess it's one of the few traits I picked up from my mother, according to him." The well of sadness whenever I talked about him felt a little less deep and murky as I spoke to Christian. I filed that information away to consider later.

"He must have been a great dad. Tell me about him." The words weren't demanding, but delivered with respect and genuine interest. My eyes pricked with hot tears.

"He was truly the best Dad ever. When I said I didn't want to fish, he never pressed but made sure I always knew the offer was open. It can't have been easy either, because my choices curtailed his. There had to be times he wanted to do things and I didn't, so he just put aside his plans. Yet, whenever I needed him, he was there."

I stared into my wine, letting the golden hue soothe the painful pit inside me. "It must have been hard when I was a teenager. A hormonal girl needing to learn about growing up and, well, you know. He made sure I had books and if I needed to talk, he was available. I can remember—" Suddenly I realized the track my memories were taken and blushed. Christian didn't need to know about the issues of puberty, single fathers, and so on.

"What?" He laid a soft hand on my shoulder and I bit my lip as that surprising zing of electricity rocketed through my body again.

"I just..." I let the words end, because whatever I was going to say would likely sound lame. Right now, my brain was warring with other parts of me, and it seemed so damned important that he thought more of me than some dumb female coming on to an older man. He had to be at least thirty, given Kira's age. I was sure he had a whole heap of experience with *that*!

"Honestly, I'd rather talk about something else right now." There. I'd done something tangible to change the topic, even if it was a classic avoidance move.

"Okay. Tell me about growing up here."

So, with the change of conversation, I let my defenses drop.

"I can't tell you the number of times I wish we'd never left the island." The words blurted out as I pushed away the bowl. Dinner had been delicious, with fresh fish and salad, topped out with a fresh fruit salad for dessert.

"Daddy, I'm tired." I could see Kira was drooping visibly. Her eyes sat at half-mast and she rubbed them.

"I should go now." I rose but Christian waved me back to my seat with a, "just give me a minute."

Wrapped in the soft emotions of well-being, I really didn't want to go. I'd enjoyed tonight, far more than I'd expected to. I rationalized those thoughts. Kira was a great kid and Christian was an entertaining host. Something else, emotions I didn't think I wanted to consider played at the edges of my mind. No matter how hard I tried to banish them, they didn't melt away on demand.

Christian returned to the room, a smile on his face. "Kira's already out for the count." The rattle of the fridge door filled the air and I smiled.

"She's a great kid."

He poured another glass of wine, then set the bottle back in the door. "Come outside. It's lovely in the breeze."

A tiny jiggle of excitement rose in my belly. I gripped the stem of my glass tightly. "You're sure I'm not overstaying my welcome?"

He turned back to me, having reached out to open the sliding glass door, and the thing that caught my attention was the shadows in his eyes. The ones I knew I was working so hard to deny.

Heat licked at my senses, warmed by the flames I'd seen dancing in his gaze.

"Come outside." He extended his hand, reaching for me. I took it, not questioning my action, and almost sighed as the warmth and electric charge pulsed through me.

*God, I really need to control my reactions.*

Outside the door, we stepped onto a long wooden veranda. He pulled me around the side, to a set of steps and into a sunken entertaining area. To the side was a large barbeque and beyond, a set of torches sunk deep into the earth. He grabbed up a small box, matches I surmised, and I heard a rasp, saw a dancing light flare.

One torch caught and the flame illuminated the area. Christian stepped up to another and lit it. A sharp wave of his hand extinguished the match and he discarded it onto the metal plate of the barbeque. "Sit down. Make yourself comfortable."

A set of four cushioned seats sat around a metal and glass table and I sank to the seat, placing my glass on the top with a tiny clink.

"I had a great day. Thanks for joining Kira and I."

I cast a look in Christian's direction, hyper aware that he'd slipped into the seat on my left.

"I really enjoyed it." I twined my fingers together, hoping to still the fidgets that rose. It wouldn't do to show just how at sea I felt right now.

"It's good for Kira to interact with other women. Peta's great with her, but she needs..." He seemed to struggle for words, but I couldn't understand why there weren't more female role models in her life.

"Surely the women you spend time with—"

His laugh cut my clumsy words off. "I don't go out with a lot of women. They seem to see a near teen as a rival." His smiled softened the words and told me he wasn't overly concerned. I couldn't quite quantify how that made me feel. So instead I inclined my head, willing him to go on. "I've learned that either they're interested or not and decided, for the most part, that I'm not overly interested in them either."

I made an 'o' with my lips. Kira was great company and I couldn't for the life of me see why anyone would begrudge the girl time with her father, or for that matter, getting to know her.

"Well, I really enjoyed her company." The second I'd spoken, I wanted to haul the comment back. Seeming forward or eager had never been my way, yet around Christian, I talked first, then worried later.

A smile broke over his face, his eyes crinkling, and a sexy, rather impudent sparkle lit his eyes. "I could tell. And I'm glad."

It took a lot of willpower to silence the gulp that nearly erupted. While the quiet reigned again I wondered, not for the first time, if he was struggling as much as I was with the pull of attraction, then shook my head at the self-absorption I'd sunk into. *It isn't all about me.*

Wind rustled through the leaves as we sat, enjoying each other's company, taking a sip from our glasses while I struggled with the mounting desire. *Control.* If only that was all it took.

Unable to stand the silence anymore, I carefully slid the glass onto the table, and he looked at me, the question in his eyes, or at least what I thought it was, pushing me to my limits. "I should go."

"Why?"

The bald question halted me. Left me considering what could be the meaning behind his words. Yet my mind existed as a pile of scrambled mush, and it took long seconds to form an answer. "Because Kira is inside, and I need to go home."

Butterflies danced in my belly, or was it quicksand? When he stood up at the same time as I did, when he reached for my hand and the silence deepened to a thick molasses that stole my ability to breathe, I gave up with a sigh. "I'm sorry, but I have to go."

The glint in his eye turned smoky and dangerous. "Do you?"

I bit my lip, knowing that I couldn't stay. Not now. Not tonight. If I did, my heart and brain warned me, I'd want more. Heaven knew, he wasn't offering anything like forever, and I dreaded the emotions I sensed would tear me apart if I settled for anything less. It was the *something* about him that continued to draw me. Been there, done that.

"I do."

"Okay then." His words married with a smile that blipped my heart rate. "But I want to explore this further." His hand waved to the area around us and I wanted to ask, needed clarification of just what he meant. Did he mean the chemistry between us?

As if he read my mind, he drew closer, both hands reaching up to catch my face between his palms. My first thought was how gentle his touch was. Then a ripple of awareness zipped through me, heating parts of me I'd thought dormant. At least until now.

Lips parted, breath colliding.

His mouth settled on mine and sensation spun in a wild flurry of color, light and need. He moved against me, his hard body against my softness, while our touch became wild.

How long we existed like that, I don't know, but when he pulled away I breathed heavily, sucking oxygen into my starved lungs while the taste of him filled my overexcited senses.

"Christian, I have to go."

I tugged away, knowing realistically I had to go now, otherwise I wouldn't. My body felt so damned heavy and liquid as hunger roared.

Unknowingly, I lifted a finger to my lip, feeling the slight swelling there, the aftereffects of that wild kiss.

I spun on my heel and headed to the house, needing to get my things and move. Anything less than determination now would undo everything I'd achieved.

In the darkness I laid on the bed, letting my mind dwell on the evening and particularly the way it ended. I could accept and acknowledge that I'd felt arousal. I could even accept that here was a man with a child. What I couldn't understand was why I felt it was so important to wait to explore everything with him.

I mean, I'd never been bothered by such conventions before. Sex was sex. Fun and somewhat satisfying, but it didn't rule my life. I certainly didn't expect it to be a long-lasting connection between us, however. Maybe I was giving it more importance that it deserved, given it had been quite a prolonged period since I'd indulged.

Sleep wisped at the corners of my consciousness and I let myself relax, fingertips releasing as I worked to let go, aware that the final thought summed up the situation more than adequately.

When I dropped to sleep, it was like a stone into water. Deep and consuming.

*"My child, you look distressed."*

*My mama, her face lined and careworn, frowned at me as she twitched the skirts of her patched gown. The one she'd worn for many years. Her everyday gown.*

*"I met a man, mama. A captain." My lips quivered on that word. My father had been a captain. A man with a woman in every port, it seemed. Like so many of the sea, more than one held the title of wife, although, only one could rightfully claim it. We'd learned that lesson well.*

*Mama's eyes welled and she seemed to stoop lower, as if the burden she carried on her soul became weightier. "Daughter, men of the sea will only stay for a short while. They don't commit to a woman like other men." I knew what she meant, after all, that was why we lived in a hovel, with holes in the roof and walls patched and re-patched.*

*The man she thought she'd married had another wife, one that was truly entitled to his name. He'd left when I was young. His real wife had found out about us and others. We'd been left in the street, after she'd screeched and ordered us out of our home. The harsh words still reverberated through my brain after so many years.*

*The woman had named me bastard, stripped us of everything we'd thought was ours, including our dignity. It was a day etched in my memory. I was grateful my sister, Maria, was too young to know of our father and the disgrace yet.*

*"He's different, Mama. I know it." I felt sure that my claim was right yet understood on a primal level why Mama would demand he prove it to her. There'd be no courting' til she satisfied her distrust.*

*For a moment I wanted to rail against the fate that had thrust this heavy burden upon us. My friends, or those I'd made in the years since our disgrace were already either promised or had taken a husband. Some already had young families of their own, and yet at nearly twenty and two I was a spinster. Alone and unmarried.*

*"Do not be so quick to accept everything he tells you. Remember what befell us before." Steel slashed her words, cold and hard. Unyielding.*

*I bowed my head, understanding her fears. "Yes, Mama. Only... Let him prove himself."*

*A sigh, heavy and full of weariness echoed. "You are so sure?"*

*"I am."*

*"Then let him come and meet with me. Only not today. I will clean first and prepare food."*

*I knew she'd see it as a matter of honor that the house and herself, not to mention the spread she offered, would be the best she could manage.*

*Money was tight and Mama made a pittance taking other women's sewing and cooking for those who had the money. She made small dainty cakes and morsels, fit for any fine house in the district and was regularly called upon for her expertise, but it didn't raise a lot.*

*I'd offered to find a way to increase our income, but Mama had spoken sternly. "No daughter of mine will seek a paid occupation while we have a choice. Your family history is long and illustrious."*

*My friendships with others in the township had already stretched her acceptance of our diminished status. I couldn't ask more, so had quietly acquiesced and studied in the hopes that one day a suitor would appear.*

*I smiled and reached for a sheet of paper and taking up the quill beside it, wrote a note to the Captain, inviting him to join us for tea on the morrow. Once sanded, I folded and sealed it with wax. Tugging on my bonnet and gloves, enfolding my good shawl around my shoulders, I set out to find a boy to deliver my missive, while hope rose in my breast. Maybe tomorrow I would begin the journey to becoming a wife.*

*When the morning came, the house shone. It might be lowly, but Mama had cleared worked through the eve and night to produce a wonder. The kitchen bore the aroma of fancies and her good gown was covered by a new hessian pinafore.*

*"Oh Mama, thank you." Thick tears gathered in my throat, nearly choking me. I knew exactly what this must cost her, but deep in my heart joy burgeoned.*

*Mama demanded I play the small harpsichord she'd accepted years ago for a favor. The measures of the melody filled the air, slightly off key, but the sounds of the minuet lifted our spirits higher. I knew I looked lovely in the pale blue gown Mama had refashioned for me. The reverend's wife had discarded it and Mama had carefully unstitched, re-cut and re-stitched it while adding new lace and ribbons.*

*At the appointed hour of two, the knock on the door had us glancing toward each other. "You answer the door, while I tidy myself."*

*I rose eagerly while Mama retired to the kitchen to straighten her gown and*

*hair, leaving the ugly apron behind. We'd already laid the food on the table,
so it gave an air of gentility.*

*Opening the door, I was amazed once more by the breadth of his shoulders,
the gleam in his eyes and how my whole body wanted to gravitate towards
him. Instead, I controlled myself, extending my hand as Mama had taught
me. "Captain, you are most welcome. Please come." I led the way, listening
as he closed the door firmly.*

*The room seemed less bright and far shabbier now that he was here and for
the first time I wanted to cringe.*

*I introduced my mother, and the captain took her hand, bowing formally.
"Ma'am."*

*Some of the starch seemed to leave her then as she led him to the seats.*

*We took tea and talked. He spoke of the sea, his ship and his family, and by
the time he took his leave, I knew Mama was, if not convinced, well on
the way.*

*"I set sail three days from now. I will visit tomorrow, if I may, and perhaps,
we could walk to the seawall and back?" He sought permission from Mama,
who gave a small nod, and I knew I wouldn't sleep a wink tonight. Then he
left us.*

Waking was like walking through molasses. Pushing
away the heaviness that invaded me, I knew I'd felt
every emotion that Alice had.

Every hint of excitement and longing had driven itself into my
psyche, connecting me to the dead woman.

Why her story was so important I didn't yet understand, but it
occurred to me that there was a reason why I was being used as the
vessel to bring about rest for this couple. I stamped down the
momentary urge to ignore her. They'd waited over a hundred years to
find their rest, so the least I could do was help them achieve it.

My feet touched the warm boards of the floor and I dragged the
light wrapper over myself, before padding to the bathroom while
considering what I'd learned. She hadn't had an easy life, starting out
with some affluence before the disaster of the other woman discov-
ering their existence.

Exhaustion dragged at me like a ball and chain. I was growing wearier with each passing night and it occurred to me something would likely give soon. "You know, it would be much easier if I could just work out what I need to do for you, then letting me fix it." There might have been a touch of asperity to my words as I concluded my ablutions, then shame filled me. After all, it wasn't their fault...

# CHAPTER 7

The sun was high in the sky by the time Christian arrived with Kira tagging along behind him. "I thought we might take a walk along the beach. We've been at this solidly for days." A smile grew on his face. "Well, except for yesterday."

Little crinkling lines feathered out from his eyes and the upturn of his lips told me he was feeling good. The urge to share my dream needed a lot of squashing down. After all, Kira was with him, so as far as I could tell that meant today was a day of rest. Besides, it was Sunday.

"Sure. Just let me grab some shoes." I looked at myself in the mirror, ran my fingers through my hair, smoothing it down. My skin had bronzed since I'd been on the island, and the highlights in my hair shone with health. The jean shorts and tank fitted perfectly and, better yet, were unstained. That was a definite plus lately, as I'd been ratting around in the shed and roof space, leaving dirty dust trails on my clothing.

We headed to the edge of the yard and through a rickety fence. Over the last week or two, I'd hacked out the old steps down to the beach, the weathered wood cracked and showed the damage of storm and sun over the years, but I'd remembered them and determined to replace, piecemeal if necessary, the rotted boards and restore my access. The sand whispered beneath our feet as we clambered down the final dune. The azure of the water twinkling like a million stars before us as it bobbed up and down.

"Daddy, can I hunt for shells?" Kira called to Christian and he turned to her, his gaze open.

"Sure, just don't get too far ahead of us."

With those words the child skipped gaily ahead, and I was reminded that she was still very young, no matter that she spoke and acted far older than her years.

"She's fantastic, Christian."

His grin nearly melted my insides. "I couldn't ask for a better kid." Then he extended his arm, his look turning far more serious. "Hold my hand?"

The melting sensation ramped up, congealing somewhere between my abdomen and another, more needy place.

Without answering, I accepted the embrace, aware that I'd somehow committed myself. It wasn't a word or even a glance that reinforced it, but the heat and sparks of electricity that arced between us.

"Let's follow Kira." We turned and followed the child who was now some distance up the deserted beach. "Tell me about last night's dream."

I glanced in his direction, wondering how he'd known.

The words fell from my lips as we meandered, stopping here and there when he'd query something. Finally when I told him every-thing, he frowned at me.

"It would have been hard, having to leave everything behind. The indignity of being thrown out like that." He sucked in a heavy breath. "I didn't know all of that, just bits and pieces. Maria wrote in later life that she'd learned the identity of her father only after she'd married and who her mother had been. I can't remember the name though."

I worried my lip. "It's really odd that I know Alice's story. It would make more sense if you understood it. I mean, you've got Maria's letters." The confusion over this didn't make any sense to me.

I gazed at the ocean, watching it curl and advance, while Kira played and giggled near us. "We don't know what caused Alice and Michael to be parted. We can guess it was official business, given the pay off the family received. Maybe if we learned more about both families, at least we can think about how they reacted. Why they chose such a remote location to set up house?"

Christian sighed. "Maybe. We could be clutching at straws but that makes as much sense right now until something else is revealed. I've got the letters at home. I can bring them by in the morning. Unless, you'd like to come for dinner?"

The curl of sensual hunger rose in me again. It seemed these days it wasn't far from the surface.

"I should really do my washing." It sounded lame. *Hell, it is lame!*

Clearly, he knew that too. "You're going to do your washing tonight?" His dry tone left me blushing.

"I should."

"If it's any consolation, Kira is heading to Peta's tonight. She's taking the whole class over to the mainland, where their teacher is running a weeklong camp. You won't be parading in front of anyone."

His words tied me in knots. I wanted to go. I really did, but that tiny bit of reserve demanded I say no.

"Of course, if you're uncomfortable, we don't have to do anything. Just talk."

Capitulation loomed.

This was a moment. One of those where you're sure the precipice is about to give under your feet. I could step back to safety or let it drop and take me where it would.

"I'd like that."

The bottom fell out of my stomach, but the satisfaction of having spoken made up for it all.

Dusk crept up on me and I glanced at the sky, watching the hues of violet and gold streak into the darkening inkiness. In my belly, a million butterflies took to wing as I swung my car down the sandy lane. The car stopped and I tugged on the handbrake before turning the key in the ignition to stop the engine.

I breathed deeply; gulping the air down into my lungs and felt them expand. I hoped it would quell my uncertainty. It didn't.

Climbing out of the car on wobbling legs, I tottered to the door, my hand grasping my bag. Secreted inside was a change of underwear and a clean top. Just in case. "Good thing this is a huge bag."

The small bit of mirth settled me, centered my mind and now I could reach for the doorknocker. I rapped once, then again. The sound of feet heading in my direction heralded Christian's answer.

When the door opened, I felt shock. Another woman stood there, blonde and trim. Her makeup carefully applied and her dress fitted in all the right places to accentuate her assets and showed as much as she could without being obscene. "Can I help you?"

In front of her, I felt shabby. "I, uh, Christian and I have..." Could I call this a date? I licked my now dry lips.

"Oh. You must be Tabitha. He told me all about you, but right now he's busy with our daughter. She had a little accident."

Her words crashed down on me. "Is Kira okay? Can I see her?"

The woman smiled, cat-like and not at all friendly. "I'm sorry. This is time for family. I'm sure you understand." She slammed the door in my face, and I stood there. Shocked and hurt to the core. Anger followed on swift wings.

I'd been cast aside like a dirty dishrag without even the benefit of an explanation?

On stiff legs, with wounded dignity cloaking me, I strode to my car, all vestiges of the butterflies and hopes extinguished.

"Damn you, Christian. You could have called me."

I slammed myself into the car, dragged the door closed behind me and tugged on the ignition key. The car stuttered, then started. I headed for home, driving a little faster than I would normally have. At my own cottage, I slammed the car door shut after alighting and stumbled up my steps.

I tugged on my clothing, stripping it from my body as I muttered and headed for the bathroom.

"I'm glad I know now." I told myself as I inspected my face in the mirror. My cheeks were red and my red-gold hair wild from the drive home, sticking out at odd points. In my eyes was hurt. Yes, his daughter was his first priority, but couldn't he have taken a moment to let me know, so I didn't turn up and... I sniffled and dashed away the tears that fell.

In that instant, I compared myself to the vision who'd answered his door and the truth shamed me. Me, of the green eyes, messy red-gold hair and deeply tanned skin. She'd been all golden blonde perfection with ivory skin and sapphire blue eyes. Who could compare us and find me the more favorable?

Where she was svelte, I was curved. Well, more than curved at that.

"So that's it. Done." I ran a shower and stepped within, letting the warm water stream over my flesh as I gave myself to the tears that had to flow. I hadn't expected that he'd committed himself to me. We'd not made any promises, but the tiny chink of deep emotion in my heart shattered. Splintered into the tiniest of shards.

I cried until my head hurt and my eyes ached. It took an effort, but I stopped myself. "He didn't promise you anything and yes, you wanted what you thought was possible. It's done. Get over it." I didn't feel better, but saying the words out loud gave me the energy to climb out of the tub, dry myself and head to the bedroom. Hunger wasn't on my radar, so going to bed seemed the best option.

*The dream surrounded me, fog winding around my legs as I looked forward. Knew I was Alice once more.*

*The ship rocking beneath my feet, as the captain steered us toward our new home. My mother had remained behind with my sister Maria. I'd felt such grief at leaving them behind, but she'd assured me that with my new husband's assistance, her situation was far more comfortable. Not that she'd accepted it without word, for she'd argued that it wasn't his place to provide for them.*

*He'd overruled her objections, made arrangements for my sister's educa-*

*tion and my mother's comfort. No longer would she be required to demean herself, working like a slave.*

*The water had been calm all day, but now night settled like a cloak, dimming the light until the hues of red and orange were replaced by obsidian, dotted with stars. "Come within, wife."*

*He stood beside me now, the small lamp illuminating us as we made our way to the cabin. It wasn't large or well furnished, but it was our home. At least until we made the island. Our furniture rested within the cargo hold, wrapped in oilcloths and crates.*

*"How much longer? When will we reach the island?"*

*Now within the cabin, and the door shut, he gathered me close. The feel of the brass buttons that dotted his jacket impressed into my gown.*

*"Within the week, my love. We make fair time and the winds are favorable."*

*I shivered, knowing that while we would be able to begin our lives anew, he'd be away often for months, sailing the seas far from me. He'd brought me here, he'd told me, because this was his home.*

*He'd painted a word picture of the cliffs, sand and sea that had brought it to life for me. His mother, he told me, lived nearby in a cottage in the village. I wouldn't be alone.*

*His fingers fluttered down the back of my gown. It gaped and I knew then, the hunger that rose within him. Its twin flame lived in me.*

*Rising to my toes, I reached up, cupping his face and drew it near to me. Our lips touched and the kiss drew my essence from deep within.*

*Wonder, the same as every time we kissed or touched, filled me. How could this man, a learned and traveled person, have never found passion and love with another woman?*

*That thought fled as he pressed me back. I stumbled, my legs catching on the wood edges of our bunk. With a breathless giggle, I fell into the soft clutches of our bedding. It cradled me as surely as my body did for my love.*

*His lips hovered above me, as if the kiss he promised wavered but a heartbeat away, then the scratching sound at the door intruded and he drew away, while I reached for the bodice of my gown.*

*"Cap'n! Dinner be ready!" The holler of the cabin steward had broken*

*the spell, and mortification nearly overcame me. I rose slowly, my hands already employed at the back of my gown.*

*"Let me." His tone was gentle. Laughter at our situation cooling the feverish warmth of my skin.*

*I rose, and he ministered to me, tending my laces with great care before gracing my rear with a gentle caress. Once again, I shivered and longed for our own home. Privacy.*

*Then he took my arm and led me to the door, and even before he opened it, gifted me with a wink.*

*I* woke with my heart beating a rapid tattoo, and every fiber in my body tense with arousal. It felt *voyeuristic.*

I knew I was dreaming as if I was Alice, but still. *"Ewww."* I couldn't control the word. "Look, I know you want me to understand what happened, but I don't need to know, see or feel that. Please don't let me dream of your...*intimacies* again!" I shuddered.

Throwing the bedclothes to the side, I noted the clock read 4:30 a.m.. Far too early to be rising, but sleep now seemed the last thing on my mind. I made a split-second decision, stripped off the clothing that had twisted around me while I slept and tugged on bathers and over the top some grungy trousers and shirt. If I couldn't sleep, I'd work.

In the old shed, I'd discovered a long-abandoned tea chest, the top firmly nailed in place. Between the adrenalin produced by the dream and the now present frustration, it seemed like a good opportunity to prise off the top and see what lay inside.

I marched to the kitchen and made coffee, then with the hammer in one hand I surveyed the box I'd shuffled into the lounge without the help of Christian. Just thinking his name reminded me of yesterday's embarrassing meeting with his ex-wife.

"Ugh! Get on with it!" The words echoed loudly, and I moved forward, the box beckoning me. The edges of the nails were driven deep into the wood, and I wondered at the best way to get the claw beneath the lid.

I tried to push the back of the hammer into the groove where the wood pieces met and failed. It slid free and I gritted my teeth, tried again.

Nothing. The claw slid free with a scrape, and I swung it up to try again. Each time I raised it; the prongs slid away, leaving another scar on the wood.

"What else do I have?" I stared at it, chewing on my thumbnail. A thought occurred and I hurried to the kitchen, ratted around in the cutlery drawer until I found an old butter knife. If I could push it in, gain enough purchase I might be able to lever the wood up enough to slide the section of hammer in.

The knife slid in partway, then stopped as if something within gripped it. "Dammit!" This time I swept up the hammer and bashed at the head of the knife, driving it further within. In the back of my mind, I realized that something inside might be in the way and I could potentially damage it.

I gave one last half-hearted whack and it pushed in, so as only the handle of the knife extruded.

Now, fully committed to my action, I started levering it up and down, listening to the creak and groan while keeping watch of the knife. The last thing I needed was for it to break.

On what felt like the seventh try, I could drag the knife free and insert the claw of the hammer. This time, when I levered the lid, the edges prized free and up; the nails screeching their resistance. I moved position, found another spot and repeated my action until finally, I could tug off the lid.

"Oh My God!"

My hand shook as I reached in, the materials dusty and deeply creased. I wondered if I should touch them. Would they crumble beneath my hand, but in the end I couldn't contain my anticipation.

I breathed over the fabrics, and a plume of dust rose.

*Cough.*

I waved away the particles and waited until my lungs stopped trying to expel the foreign matter. I sucked in a breath, held it, and reached.

This time I tugged on the gown. The material was heavy with substantial threads running through it. It reminded me of a high-quality silk. The lacework looked both intricate and delicate, so I decided not to touch that. With care, I lay it on the ground and reached in again. Another gown, of a dirty gray emerged, the buttons marching down the bodice like tiny soldier hats.

Peering into the box again, I found a wad of letters tied with an old faded blue ribbon. Unable to help myself, I pulled them out and laid them on the table. More clothing lay beneath and a hat, battered and flattened, its sad feather a threadbare stick told me they'd been a long time in storage.

These were the clothes of Alice. I knew it, because I'd seen her wearing this gray gown—I'd been wearing this gown—in my dream.

The letters called to me, as if I knew they'd contain some great important secret. "I should call Christian."

I vacillated and looked out. Dawn had risen while I'd been busy. The sun reaching, long fingers extending toward me, into the house and warming it after the cool of night.

I should let him know, but he'd no doubt be busy with Kira and his ex-wife. That tiny shard of pain decided me.

Scooping the letters up, I headed for the lounge chair and settled in. The parchment was heavy and I carefully unfolded them all, one at a time. They'd be dated, and it made more sense to read them in order, I told myself. They were, as expected, chronologically piled.

Some of them contained items and I made a notation in the tiny notepad I'd taken to keeping by the chair. One held a lock of hair, another a slip of material. The last held a battered gold ring. My stomach quavered at the sight of it. I brushed it with the tip of my finger. A shimmer of something rippled through my body. A single tear dripped down my cheek, emotions I couldn't contain welled up and I needed a moment.

With care, I laid the item aside and reached for the missives.

Once I had them in date order, I began reading.

*My dearest Alice*

*How I wish you were here. Today it's raining and the sun seems to have lost some of its brightness. Maria sits at the harpsichord. Her skill is improving daily, but I miss the gentle tones you would play as I sewed.*
*I am pleased you have arrived safely. ...*

I scanned the letter, seeking something that stood out. Something that might have a clue to the puzzle of why and where the captain had disappeared, but it was filled with talk of village life, Maria's education and how she now spent her days.

Alice's mother had written religiously, if the pile of letters was anything to go by. I made my way through the first dozen, but while I learned interesting snippets about how to darn a sock and the cooking of beef, there seemed no clue.

I pushed the read letters to the side. I'd come back to them later and maybe transcribe some of the information, but for now, my stomach rumbled, and my bladder told me I'd been there some time. So did the stiffness of my back and arms.

I rose and felt surprise when I looked at the old clock on the sideboard. I'd been up and about for over four hours. Where had the time gone?

"You know exactly where it's gone, Tabs. Now bathroom, then breakfast." I hobbled until the muscles in my legs relented and by the time I was sitting at the table with toast and coffee, I almost felt normal again.

I was clearing away and getting ready to wash up when the sound of an engine caught my attention. It didn't sound like Christian's and I hoped it wasn't that woman. The butterflies I'd felt last evening took flight again in my belly as I trudged to the door. Peering through the screen, surprise filled me. "Peta!"

The woman was dressed in tidy jeans and boots, and a tank top, looking just as tanned and capable as the last time I'd seen her.

"Christian asked me to drop by."

The bottom fell out of my stomach. "Is Kira okay?"

She stopped at the bottom step, looking uncertain, a frown

creasing her forehead.

I waved her in front of me. "Come in and have a cup of coffee?"

She nodded, bounded up the stairs and as soon as she was within my house whirled around, gripping my shoulders. "I wish you'd been there. *She* came as soon as Christian called. Kira broke her leg late yesterday, swinging on the rail at home. He had to call her, but none of us thought she'd actually turn up!"

I heard the way Peta described Christian's ex-wife, the disgust and surprise. "Umm Jan just turned up?"

"Janet," Peta corrected me absently, scanning the room. "Janet's a bitch. Only married Christian because she thought he'd someday be rich and famous, just like the guy who found the Titanic. She learned though that there isn't a lot of money unless you get into industrial salvage. And Christian never had any interest in that." She saw the pile of letters on the table and her face lit up. "You found more stuff?"

"Uh yeah. It was in a box I found in the shed. I should have waited but—"

"Oh, I know exactly what you mean. What have you found out?" She turned to me, her eyes glittering with interest.

"How to cook beef and the best thread for darning socks."

Peta's laugh tinkled and settled some of the lingering pain that I didn't realize had lodged in my chest.

"Anyway, Janet turned up yesterday. Threw her weight around and pissed Christian off big time. Told him she'd made some big mistake and really should never have left him and Kira." The whirlwind of information crashed down on me.

*Christian hadn't known she was turning up. He hadn't asked Janet for personal reasons, just because of Kira.* The weight in my chest lifted.

"Anyway, he said you'd arranged a meeting," Peta grinned at me and I had the suspicion she knew what I'd packed into my tote for our assignation. "He wanted to let you know he would have rung, but once Janet arrived there wasn't time. It was only this morning he was able to get hold of me and explain. He wants to let you know that it means nothing more than what's best for Kira."

Peta reached out, grabbed my hand and patted it. "She'll be gone soon. She never stays for more than a day or two, then we can all get back to normal."

"What about Kira?" I couldn't help myself. The poor kid in the middle of this mess would not be happy once her mother left.

"Kira knows her mother well, already. I doubt she expects much, 'cause Janet has never been the maternal type. I feel bad for Kira. We all do, so work hard to ensure she knows she's loved."

I pondered her words as I wandered into the kitchen, aware she'd be following me.

Mechanically, I heated the water, grabbed two cups and spooned the granulated coffee.

"You know, I've never seen him so interested in a woman before. He wasn't even like this with Janet. She was an aberration. The only reason they married was because of Kira, and even that didn't go quite as planned. She'd ditched them both within two years."

Honestly, I wasn't sure I wanted to hear this. The intrusion into his private life discomforted me.

"Do you want sugar?" I met her gaze and she smiled, as if understanding I needed to change the subject.

"No. Just as it comes."

We sat down; silence once more filling the room. "So, you captain a ship?"

She burbled with laughter. "It's not what I do every day. The rest of the time I'm an admin officer for the council. I work in the little office here on the island three days a week."

I blinked. "Really?"

"Well, there's only so much sailing a woman can do before it interferes with man hunting." For a moment I was shocked, thinking she was serious, but the grin that curved her lips had me shaking my head. "Actually, I'm getting married next year."

I glanced at her hand, which was bare.

"I don't wear my ring often." Peta tugged her chain from beneath her shirt.

"Oh, wow!" I looked closely and felt a ripple of shock. I'd seen the glint of that ring on Alice's finger. "That's..."

"Liam found it in an antique shop. It drew us both, so..."

My lips dried and I licked them. "That's ummm... I know that ring."

Peta cocked her head. "Alice's?"

Shock stilled me. "You know?"

"Remember, I lived with Christian until he married Janet. He'd tell me about his dreams. All about Alice. But when I saw this ring... Let's just say I felt such an affinity for it, so when it came to choosing an engagement ring, I couldn't go past it."

I shook my head. This whole situation was seriously getting stranger by the moment. "You said Christian has dreams?"

"Yeah. It seems there's one person every generation. Mom did too." Now Peta leaned forward, searching my face. Her eyes moving over my face and I just knew she was looking for confirmation I was aware of what she thought. "You're not surprised, are you?"

"Oh, I am. Very. But not for the reason you think."

Peta sat back in her chair. "Why?"

It was a bald question. One I really wasn't sure I wanted to answer, so I took a moment and considered the why's and wherefores'. "How long has Christian been dreaming?" I needed time and another question would surely give me at least a breather.

"Since adolescence." She steepled her fingers. "So?"

Now I moistened my lips. Even though she was clearly aware of what was going on, I'd be telling her something that would make the average person look at me like I was nuts. "I've uh... I dream too."

"Ah. That explains a lot."

"What does it explain?"

"Why he seems so attuned to your story. Why he didn't question what you told him. Why the tie between you has become so deep really quickly." Peta reached out a hand and I looked at it before accepting the embrace.

"You don't?"

"No. I've never felt any real connection like he does. Maybe it's best that way." Peta shrugged her shoulders.

"Ahh..."

## CHAPTER 8

*D*ays passed, and I'd finished making my way through the letters, writing notes to myself so I could find the paragraphs I needed to keep track of when the sound of an engine caught my attention. After Peta had left, I'd finished sorting through the box. At the very bottom lay a tiny case, containing a key tied to a blue ribbon. It didn't matter how much I scratched my head and searched, I couldn't work out what it belonged to. I'd already tried all the doors here in the house. I shrugged as I rose to investigate the sound on the driveway.

*Peta, again!*

I rose and made my way to the door, only to stop. *Oh, God!* Christian. I hadn't seen him since Kira's accident. So much had happened, yet only a few days had passed. I looked down and a hot red tide crept up my neck and face. Old clothes covered in dust.

I mentally compared myself to Janet and sighed. "No time to change."

He loped up the path and stood at the bottom of the steps as I stepped through the open door.

"Uh, Tabitha. I'm sorry about the other day."

Cocking my head to the side, I waited for him to continue. He stepped from left foot to right, a lock of sandy blonde hair dropping over his forehead, and he squinted at me. "I honestly didn't think Janet would come. She's never done so before."

"Hi Christian." I couldn't think of anything else to say that wouldn't sound catty or even vaguely unsettled. I really wanted to tell him how off kilter I felt, but right now, I couldn't afford to open myself further. I'd been hurt already, and that shamed me.

"Can I come in?" The hesitancy in his voice made me realize I was making him stand in the sun, like an unwelcome Jehovah's Witness.

I sidestepped wordlessly and he entered the house.

"You've been busy?"

"Yeah, I... I opened another box. There were letters from Alice's mother and..." I shrugged feeling at sea.

"Tabs, I wish Janet hadn't turned up."

I bit my lip, feeling uncertain and a little grubby with the whole *I-didn't-want-her-there* scenario playing out in front of me. I mean, she was his ex-wife and Kira's mother. "It's okay." My voice emerged kind of rusty sounding and he growled, strode forward and grabbed my shoulders.

When my gaze connected with his, the breath inside me froze. I felt shattered by the hunger that raged in the depths of his eyes. "I wanted you. I still want you." He exhaled, chest rising and falling. I felt the movement of his shirt against my body along with the warm liquid air that caressed my skin. "I dream about you."

A slight movement tugged me closer, so our lips touched. It wasn't electricity so much as magic that captured me. I was entranced by him. The warmth of his body, the heat of his passion. It pushed me beyond needy to desperate and frenzied with hunger. My ability to think vanished, sucked in by the urgency that swirled around us.

I opened my mouth to him. Let him fill me intimately, tongues dueling. My lungs burned as oxygen expired and I tugged away, needing to drag in a deep breath.

"I can't..." Tears filled my eyes as I argued with myself. *What the hell am I doing?*

"I want you on so many levels, Tabitha. I know you're questioning that right now, after Janet's appearance, but don't let that fool you.

What is between us is only the beginning. I'm not prepared to walk away from what exists here."

His words filled the empty space inside me. Did I want what he was offering? Oh yes, I did.

"I want you too. But I'm unsure. To be honest, I don't know if I can trust myself. I mean, how much of this is us and how much is the Captain and Alice? I have to wonder that there isn't some kind of *hocus-pocus kick-back.*"

My words startled him. He gave me a look I took to mean he was surprised. His eyebrows arched, his mouth dropped open, and the wide-eyed gaze told me I was on the money.

It was true. I hadn't allowed myself to voice these thoughts before now. I'd avoided these ugly truths, but with Janet and Kira in the mix, it was time to face them squarely. I had to be honest with myself and Christian.

"I—"

"It's not for me." His words crashed through the morass of whatever I'd been about to say. "I've been in a relationship before that wasn't what I needed. I've felt the connection between the Captain and Alice, but it doesn't feel like what I experience every time I'm around you. I don't have the words to explain, but it's like the emotions are darker. Heavier." He shrugged. "Like I said, no words to explain it." He gripped my hand and tugged me to the lounge chair, where I sank into the seat. "When I wanted Janet, I was sure it was right, but to be honest, looking back, it's a mystery why I thought that was true love. I mean, we connected sort-of, but not like this."

I stared at him, wondering how he could exactly quantify the problems I was struggling with.

"Christian, I want this to work so much that I ache. But there's so much that's going on, that I'm just not sure. I need time."

"I'll give you time, but Tabs, I want you to understand that this, whatever it is between us, is as essential to me as the oxygen I'm breathing."

He pulled me close, right up against his chest, and enveloped me in a strong hug. It soothed the raggedness of my emotions and gave me a feeling of belonging.

When he sighed and let me go, I wanted to burrow back into the embrace. Instead, he stood. "I don't suppose you'd offer me a coffee. We can just talk, you know."

I laughed a hiccup and shook my head. "I have lots to tell you."

*A*fter Christian left, I looked at the little house and decided I really needed some time out. We'd talked about the letters and I showed him the stash. He'd exclaimed over the gowns and encouraged my note making. Then he'd left.

I was grateful, truly, because now I had time alone to concentrate on what I knew. What I'd acknowledged. I headed for the beach.

I walked, my feet *swooshing* in the sand as I contemplated the situation of what we knew about Alice and her Captain. I now understood her inner motivation and acceptance of the long distance between home and here. "But what is it that keeps you apart, dammit?"

Sliding my cupped hand over my brow, I searched the horizon but there were no answers there. I didn't even know the damned question to ask, let alone how to find the answers. I sat down, letting the sand conform around my body, so I was cradled. I tugged my hat down low, to look over the bridge of my nose.

The warmth of the day lulled me, the noise of lapping water a lullaby, and I drifted away.

*"T*abitha. Time is running short. You must help us." The captain implored me, and I frowned.

*"I don't know how. You haven't given me anything I can work with. There're no answers or questions that are leading me in the right direction."*

*He growled and reached to me. I felt him, his skin cool and firm. "The letters. They are the first clue. Read them. Dissect them. It's all there."*

*The letters from Alice. I bit my lip and felt the sting. "But they talk about mundane things. Day-to-day actions interspersed with some gossip. I don't know—"*

*"Read them, because the answer is there. Time is short. My spirit is failing, as is Alice's. I cannot reach her, and she is locked from you too. You must find her before we fade."*

*Then he did just that, not slowly as I'd become accustomed to, but one moment he was there, then he was gone. I stood there in the gray silence, lost and alone. A sense of doom and danger permeated the air. My breath clogged in my throat and I choked.*

*"Hello?" My heartbeat sped up as fear trickled through my veins. I tried to step, but something dragged at me, I hadn't noticed it, but now I couldn't move. It held me immobile.*

*The more I tugged and pulled, the further into the mire I sank. "Oh, God!" I bent down, looking for some clue as to what kept me here. Nothing except dark and damp.*

*"I need to get out." The wetness seeped up until it finally crept up around my shoulders. "Let me go!" My scream echoed...*

*T*he gentle lapping of the wave woke me and I looked down to see it rising around me.

"Oh my God!" I pushed away the sand, though it sucked me into itself. The release came with a wet suction-like sound. I stood and wiped as much of the wet mess off me as I could, then made back to the house, while memories of the impassioned warning from the Captain played in my head. But the whole time, I was aware of a sensation of being watched. Dark. Overwhelming.

I bit my lip and scurried inside. Only then did it dissipate.

I needed to read the letters, but now, maybe I needed Christian's input? *Perhaps he'd be able to shed some light on the problem?*

Gazing through the window, I noted the haziness of dusk had started to paint the sky in shades of violet and blues.

Too late tonight. "Tomorrow. I'll collect everything up and talk to him."

It didn't matter though that my planning made sense. There was now a sense of urgency—one I hadn't experienced before—pushing me on.

I told myself it made no sense, even as the sound of an engine filled the air.

I wandered to the front of the house and peered around. The car drawing up was black and new. Sleek lines and, to my fevered brain, vicious looking.

A man in a suit climbed out, and while I could see another person within the dark tinting obscured who it was and whether a man or a woman.

I waited in the shadows, the chill of the air nipping at my skin. "Hello? Anyone there?"

I didn't respond to the hail. Just waited and watched.

The man stumped in the direction of the steps and I drew back, thankful that the shadows hid me.

The whole situation felt wrong. A chill ricocheted through me and I fancifully had the impression it was all to do with him, not the cool evening air and shadows surrounding me.

He carried a yellow-brown envelope, the sort that usually declared official documents, and peered through the door. "Hello? Anyone home?"

I observed him standing there for several brief minutes before he turned with a sigh and headed back for the car. Even as he opened the door he was talking to the person within. "No one there. I'll have to try again tomorrow."

The low tones murmured, and he shook his head. "No. These documents must be hand delivered to be legal. I can't just leave them. After all, this is about dissolving the legal ties to the property."

His words as he climbed into the sedan stole my breath. *Dissolve the legal ties to the property.* Was this the reason for the Captain's urgency? Was this why everything was happening?

Under normal circumstances I'd say it was ridiculous and made no sense, but then, none of this situation could even remotely be called usual or rational.

I waited for the glow of the taillights to disappear before I emerged from the darkness.

"They can't take my home." The words melted into the air, nothing more than a quavering echo.

Clearly, I needed help, and I needed it now! On that thought, I sprinted for the kitchen and snatched up the phone. My fingers stabbed at the keypad and I entered Christian's number.

"Hello?"

"It's me and I need your help." The waver in my voice echoed and I heard his indrawn breath.

"Are you safe? I'm on my way."

"Yes, but please hurry."

Once he'd hung up and the beeping line told me the call was disconnected, I slumped against the counter.

I wasn't being overly dramatic. Was I?

Christian's car pulled up to a screeching stop outside my house. I watched as he flung himself out and slammed the car door closed. I curled my hand around the doorknob even as he sprinted up the front steps.

"Christian." The words were so much more than a greeting. His gaze roamed over me, no doubt taking in my disheveled and soggy state. I hadn't changed and the sand stained and still damp, together with my wild-eyed stare stopped him in his tracks.

"What's wrong?" He peered around the room, the gloom only illuminated by the phone in my hand and the moonlight.

"Oh God. There was a man here. They want to dissolve my ownership of the property." I went on to tell him what I'd seen and heard. Then I stopped and bit my lip.

"But why?"

Christian slid his arm around me, and I curled in, desperately yearning the warmth there.

I told him about my dream and the urgency I'd sensed, and he grunted, fingers flexing on my shoulders. "Grab everything you have and some clothes. You're coming home with me and we'll go through every book and paper. There must be a clue somewhere."

"I don't—"

"Dammit, don't think, woman. We need to solve this puzzle and clearly time is short. Tell me what you need and where these things are, and get some clothes together."

I'd never been attracted to domineering men before, but damn, Christian's words filled me with heat. My body clenched, hard. Time seemed to pause as I stared at him. "Go." That was just what I needed to hear, and it carried enough authority that I stopped wasting time. The tension between us continued, yet the impossible web released me enough that I could react.

"There's the large chest in the kitchen. It's got the letters and my notepad is on the table. I shouldn't need anything else tonight."

He grunted and made for the doorway while I hurried to the bedroom. I grimaced, catching sight of myself in the mirror. I was wild haired and messy. "Two seconds." Of course no one was there to hear my words, but they steadied me as I stripped down, tugging off panties and bra and riffled through my drawer. A sound caught my attention and I spun, startled to find Christian in the doorway, an arrested expression on his face. His face suddenly harsh and the skin of his cheeks stretching tight.

"I should—" His strangled words told me of his embarrassment at catching me naked, the red tide cresting his neck reinforcing my deduction.

His eyes though told the story of his desire. They roamed over my body, dilated and hungry.

Whatever sound I made, and I'm sure it was a hungry moan as my body reacted to the urgent desire, broke his concentration and he stepped back. "I'll let you dress."

For a second, neither of us spoke a word, but he knew then, I'm sure, that I shared his hunger. Spinning away, I reached for clean clothing and tugged it over my now highly aroused body. Every slide and pull reminded me of what I needed, and my body thrummed.

God knows the sound of his footsteps, his retreat, didn't lessen the dragging claw of need that tore at my psyche. It bit deep and gripped on.

Slumping to the bed, I dragged a shaking hand over my face. "Something is seriously going to have to give."

One breath, then another filled my lungs. The act of clearing my mind required concentration, but I welcomed it as the fog cleared, marginally.

Once I could think again, I rose, determined to grab the clothing and get out of there. Without thought, I tugged at underwear, pajamas, a t-shirt and shorts. Just enough for an overnight visit.

I stuffed them in the tote bag I'd dropped by the bed the other night and scooped it up. In my mind, I thought over my needs from the bathroom. Toothbrush, hairbrush, deodorant. Only the essentials. Dropping them into the toiletry bag and stashing it gave me a couple of precious more seconds, then I continued to the lounge where Christian waited.

At the doorway, I stilled. He stood, stiff and silent, facing the front door. A statue was probably more welcoming right now, and I sighed. Not only could I understand his tension, I shared it. The situation between us was creating a problem, and I really wished we could avoid it.

When Christian turned, the mass in my stomach returned to a lava-like consistency.

"I can't make you any promises that I won't—"

I knew what he meant and shook my head, stopping his words, then I reached out and placed a single finger flat against his lips. "I know. I accept that."

A little of the stiffness leached from him, as if I'd released a pressure valve within his body. The storm that had started raging once more inside me abated a little, allowing me to think and acknowledge that tonight I would likely cross my personal line.

"Then we should get out of here."

With a quick slide, I gathered up my keys, while hitching the tote over my shoulder.

# CHAPTER 9

*C*radling the coffee while we talked, I reflected on the evening.

Kira was at Peta's so we spread the letters out over the table, aware we wouldn't be interrupted. I read the notes out loud and watched as Christian tapped information onto the small laptop in front of him.

"And they were definitely in Cornwall at the time of the marriage?" His words demanded answers I couldn't be sure of.

"All I can see is that the letters at the top are tagged as Cornwall, but I honestly don't know. It's not something that's ever been talked of." I flipped through the pieces of parchment, but there was no definitive answer. Not for the first time, I wished I could ask my father what he knew, had read or been told. Now I was aware I had no member of my family to talk to. It had been him and I for so long. "That doesn't mean anything, does it?"

Christian relaxed back, stretching and crossing his arms behind his head.

"But that wouldn't really have much impact—"

The look he shot me was surprised. "Of course it could. It would depend on who gifted the continuous occupation of your family to the land. I know you have a letter from the Government but—"

At Christian's assertion, I made a claw of my fingers and dug them into my hair, needing to feel the pain so it might outweigh the frustration. "Aargh!" Then I slumped. "Look, I don't know the answers. I don't even know where to find them." I let my head rest on the wooden tabletop, my hands flopping down to the wood with a *thunk* and accepted I was in over my head.

"I do."

Two words, yet they stilled me and the angst that was rapidly growing.

"And you didn't think to say anything?" My words were muffled, lips to the wood as I thought. *He'd never said anything, so why wait until now?*

I breathed in and out, focusing on the act that usually required no thought or effort before.

"What do you know?"

"Well, I happen to have connections. People in places, that kind of thing."

I growled and he gave a chuckle.

"Tell me."

"Well, in my job, I know people who know people. As it happens, one of my old college buddies works in archives and I asked him to have a look at what he could find. There wasn't much, except..."

I bit my lip as his words died away. "What?"

"There's a Torrens Title."

That didn't mean anything to me, and I shook my head. "A what? What's a Torrens title?"

"Well way back, title changes and information required information, letters, inventories and copies of wills to be attached. They called them a Torrens Title. This one has a Torrens Title and there's a notation that a packet of information should be with it. However, it's not in the normal archives. Or the title is, but not the package. It seems because of services rendered to the crown, it was stored in another, more secure location."

I frowned; the whole situation felt odder than ever. "Where?"

"The Colonial Office."

I'd heard that term before. "Isn't that in London? I mean, that makes it super official, right?"

"Yes. But that opens a new set of issues. See, because a lot of documents that were belonging to the Colonial Office were destroyed in World War Two, our best bet is to find someone who can locate it, *if* the packet still exists."

I slumped in my chair, letting every muscle relax as the enormity of the situation impinged on my mind. Documents that could potentially explain how the land had come to pass into my family might have been destroyed. The government wishing to resume the ownership of the land, a ghost or two seeking peace. "Oh man!" I swiped my shaking hand over my brow, noting the sweat that had built up. "Never a dull moment in my life."

# CHAPTER 10

*W*e finally mounded up the documents and pushed away from the table sometime after ten p.m.. "Can I offer you a glass of wine?"

I trembled, because in his voice there was so much more than just an offer of a drink. I read it in the gleam in his eyes, the way his hand glanced over mine. He drew closer and my breath fled.

"I... Yes, that would be lovely."

His smile warmed me all the way to the tips of my toes and I blushed, the heat leaving my ears pulsing along with the skin of my face and neck.

"I'll be right back." The way he spoke, the timbre of his voice so deep had other parts of my body tingling.

I didn't turn to watch him head for the fridge. The situation felt downright intimate, and yes, that intimidated me.

When he returned with a glass and slid it into my hands I murmured, "thanks," and headed for the open doors. On the veranda, I settled against the bannister and gazed into the dark night. In the distance, purple-red lightning flared.

Christian followed, his footsteps stopping just beside me. I could look at him, in fact, I probably should have but the trembling of my legs told me to take a moment. So I did.

"Tabs." His voice caressed me.

"Christian." My turn was slow, just like the hard thud of my heart.

"I want you." His eyes shone in the dark, his words honest as they echoed his hunger. A hunger matched by the fire deep within me.

When he reached up and stroked my cheek with his free hand, I leaned in, felt the warmth of his touch.

For an instant I hovered, swayed towards him, then he stepped closer, so that our breaths mingled. "Tabitha, I want you now. Tonight. Will you be with me?"

In answer, I leaned in and kissed him.

I wanted to gift him with a tender graze. A thank you for being so understanding while I still had questions that remained unanswered; yet it swiftly turned hot. Lips slanting and dragging eagerly against each other. He demanded entry to my mouth, and I capitulated, so his tongue speared deeply in a parody of the most awesome intimacy.

A wet feeling dragged my mind back to the here and now, and I gasped. My wine tipped down my clothing. I gave an embarrassed laugh, but Christian merely removed the glass from my slack hand.

"Come." He spoke in a gravelly voice that scored my mind.

I followed.

He stilled in the kitchen, draining the last of the wine from his glass as he watched me, the draught making his throat work, and I swallowed convulsively as each movement fanned the heat inside me to a wicked blaze.

"Christian?" I don't know what I was asking. Was it, do you want me, or could it have been a request for more? I didn't care, as I existed on a plane of pure heat and hunger.

He slid the glass to the counter where it joined mine. I'd barely noticed him place it there, lost in the magic he wove around me.

Now, when he advanced, I knew and understood the question I'd declined to answer. He slid a hand beneath my legs, claimed my lips and lifted me against his chest. The need to twine my hands around his neck and tug him closer, so my body connected with him was overwhelming.

The kiss was hungry. He gorged like a starving man and I gave him everything. On some dim level, I'm sure I almost offered him my very soul.

When we reached his room, he slid me to the bed, the soft comforter a counterpoint to the hardness of his body.

Stepping away left me empty.

I yearned for him and watched, starved as he stripped before me. My own hands worked quickly, loosening clips and buttons, flinging my bra to the floor. Then, gloriously naked, we came together: the rasp of his chest hair against my sensitized nipples had me gasping.

I needed more and dug fingers into his shoulders, clawing and dragging. I pulled away, chest burning with oxygen deprivation.

"Christian, please..."

He understood my need. "I can't be slow. Not this time, God help me."

He crawled over me, splayed my legs with eager movements while his hands explored the dips and hollows of my body. My breasts swelled as my sex melted into a drenched puddle of erotic neediness.

"I need to be inside you."

I gasped as his fingers found the entry to my overheated sex, while another finger skated over my clit. I bowed up, unable to help myself, fingers burrowing into the comforter.

"Christian!"

Then he was there, nudging my legs open and sliding oh so slowly within my body.

Friction, heat and wetness allowed him to enter easily. Thoughts fled as my body splintered, the orgasm screaming over me. I saw stars then blackness as I lost touch with reality before returning to myself. It took a monumental effort to reopen the eyes I must have shut during the waves of pleasure.

He moved over and above me, sliding in and out before he grunted and gave one last heave. I felt the sensation of his jetting. His body stilled, held in the act of pleasure. Eyes closed and sweat running in rivulets down his chest.

One drop landed on my skin, cooling my flesh, and that brought me back to reality fully. *Sensation.*

He slumped over me, heavy and boneless.

I slid my hand around his waist, holding him close for just a little longer. My fingers painting circles as I considered the gift he'd given me. Pleasure. The feel of him...

Awareness flashed. "*Ohmygod!* We didn't use a condom." I pushed at him, felt the tension seize his body. What had I done? What had we done?

"Tabs, I'm sorry."

I glanced at his bone-white features. Neither of us had been thinking. We'd just lost ourselves in the moment. But consequences... I counted, trying to be rational. When had my last period been?

It took time for Christian to calm my fears. Although I'd nearly abandoned him at that point, he'd encouraged me to shower, have a warm milk and settle in, daggy pajamas and all.

The fear that I'd made a huge mistake rode me, but the reality was I knew there wasn't anything I could do until morning.

When the sun had risen, so did I. Christian still slept and I wasn't sure of the protocol for the morning after, particularly under these circumstances. Instead, I headed for the kitchen and perked a coffee. I was outside, on the veranda when he came to me...

*Shadows parted and there he stood, an imposing man in a Captain's uniform. The dark blue with gold buttons. "Tabitha, you have veered away from the path I set you. Why?" He frowned and I had to search deep within me for the honest answer he deserved.*

*Even as I considered his words, I understood the Captain's concern. "I didn't mean to, but they came yesterday to resume the property. I was upset. I'm not even sure if I have made a very big mistake or not."*

*"Who came?" He frowned at me, a deeply unsettling visage.*

*"Someone from the government. I don't know what's changed, but it makes no sense." I bit my lip. "We've been working on learning why you were granted the parcel of land. Can you clarify this at all?"*

*Sadness filled his eyes. "If I could, I would. But in death as in life, I am bound. I cannot speak of that which gave you such an inheritance, only that you must find it soon. I fear another, with the power of—" his eyes bulged, and he grayed, seeming less substantial than before. "I say too much and pay for my openness." He rubbed at his chest, gasping a little. "You must seek those, which would steal your future, my child. Take heed. You've found much which will aid you."*

As if he'd outstayed his welcome, his form started to wither as a cold wind swirled around me.

When I came back to myself, I was chilled to the bone, huddled in the chair, my face resting on the side of the house.

"Tabitha?"

Christian spoke and I jumped, spooked by his sudden presence. "Oh, Christian. He was here. The Captain. He says we've found most of..."

"Later. Come inside." His eyes crinkled and lips pulled tight.

"What's wrong?" Should I reach out and touch him, or should I keep my hand to myself. The morning after confusion filled me. I didn't know how to respond to his sudden change of demeanor.

"Please." He stepped back and slid open the glass door, making way for me to pass in front of him.

Christian held out a hand, one that had caressed my skin only hours earlier, and I felt like there was a disconnect between us. It was as if he were a stranger. I swallowed and continued down the hall to the front room in the house. There on the seat sat the ex-wife, and in her hand, she held an envelope.

"Oh." Janet spoke faintly, her eyes running up and down my body with a sneer before dismissing me. "It's early for company, Christian."

Shame flared, just like the blush that heated my skin. "I'll just..." I waved and made to step away, but Christian caught my hand.

"Stay."

"Really, Christian—"

"I don't want to interrupt—" We both spoke at the same time, but he shook his head.

"No. Janet, I want you to tell Tabitha what you're doing and why you're here."

She colored now, an awkward crimson. "Really, Christian. I don't want to..."

"I'm not willing to wait, Janet. Tell her what you're here to do."

She turned, anger and an even more insidious emotion present in the tension that surrounded her. "Well, I came to deliver a letter." With ill grace, Janet thrust it in my direction before spinning to face Christian. "Done."

She stepped away, but Christian thrust out a hand. "Not so fast. Tell her."

The tension was replaced by cold stony anger. "You don't get to tell me—"

"Oh, can it, Janet." Exasperation dripped from his words. "It's time to act like the grown up you only pretend to be. Now tell Tabitha what's in that letter."

I bit my lip. If Christian was as angry as it seemed, I'd want to know sooner rather than later. "I don't understand." Confusion and fear bloomed in my chest. What could Janet possibly have to say to me? I mean, it made no sense.

"Your home is being resumed. The letter there, details all the information you need to know."

On that, Janet whirled and left the room, followed by Christian who remonstrated loudly. It didn't impinge on me though. I was numb. My home. Mine. *Resumed.*

Anger coursed through my veins. "Over my dead body." I whirled, heading for the bedroom where I'd stashed my things. Christian clearly knew something last night. After all, he'd whisked me away long before I could get my head around what had happened.

Betrayal ran deep. The words of dad's letter came to me. Like a warning that no matter what we thought, we had to be careful who we told.

*It may answer some questions and raise others. It's the way of our line. There are questions. My mother said sometimes at dawn she'd smell burning like that of gas, but she never found the source. My grandfather claimed there were spirits involved and awareness of them would be the greatest armor I could have. I don't know so much about that, yet, he always claimed, when I spent time with him as a child down on the beach where he would talk to me of my heritage, that the task one of us undertook would be dangerous. I never felt that, yet you were always so much more open and that is the reason I mention the times you knew things were about to happen. Even as a child, your dreams, the ones we never discussed with your mother, worried me. It's why I made the decision to move you. I had hoped you would be able to grow before dealing with the secrets of our line.*

*Above all, though, others not of the family will never understand. They will question your sanity if you tell them. Be wary.*

I hunted and groped, finally everything I'd removed last night stashed in the large bag. I clambered up to find him standing in the doorway. "Tabitha?"

His eyes were shadowed. Cautious. I didn't care. "I'm going."

He stared at me. "Why?"

"Because I have to concentrate. Work out what's happening and why. I need to do this alone." And I did. I couldn't lean on him. I couldn't rely on anyone except myself. Asking for assistance would mean I'd need to let go of my control—and heavens knew control was what had got me through my father's death and everything else since. I needed control like a baby needed a security blanket. Hell, it was my security blanket!

"Tabitha..." He stopped, looked at my face and grimaced.

"I have to go."

My mind was a confused jumble, trying desperately to deal with the shocks that had occurred in the last twelve hours. The love-making—sex, I reminded myself—the truth about Janet and the people at my house. Besides, on top of all that, I owed the Captain and his Alice my whole efforts to sort out what happened to him and somehow try to bring them back together and fix whatever kept them apart.

A big job. But I'd promised.

The house lay silent as I stumped back up the steps, shoved open the door and dropped my bag to the floor with a thump. I stood in the doorway, surveying the room. And the sense of loneliness was all-pervasive.

*What the hell am I doing?* Tears burned my eyes. "I'm being an adult. Making a choice to focus on what I need to do." The echo of my words didn't in any way make me feel better.

The box under my arm was heavy and I trudged to the table and carefully placed it down. I felt the scorch of a tear trickle down my face. It dripped onto the cardboard, splattered, and I stared for a second before I swiped at it. The dark mark from the tear remained. "Just like my life."

With a sigh, I wiped the moisture from my face and dropped into the seat, pulled the box closer.

Pushing back the flaps felt like opening the pandora's box that best described my life.

I picked up the notes I'd made. No time like the present to drop back into the research. Time was running short.

*"Tabitha."* I knew that voice. I glanced up. The shadowy form of a woman wavered before me. *"Time is short. I cannot help much, but you must seek the letters hidden. They are—"* Ghostly Alice glanced over her shoulder as if she were hiding. When she looked back at me, I read fear. Her lips moved, but I couldn't hear her.

"Where?" I leaned forward, hoping to catch a sound, even a whisper. Without warning, she was gone.

"Bloody secrets!" My voice echoed through the house. Strident. Angry. I pushed away and up from the table. "I don't know where to look. You haven't given me enough to go on, and I don't know where to start."

As quickly as my fury surged, it was gone, leaving me drained. "I can't do this." The truth was, I was out of my depth. I didn't have any clue where to go or what to do next. The only clue was those words. *Hidden.*

"Huh. If I was looking for something hidden, where would I start?" I glanced around the kitchen, for the first time questioning everything I knew about the history of this place. The house was old —or at least the main, middle section. That's where I'd start.

I prowled the room, searching for visual clues. "Not enough," I muttered, dragging at the lounge. "There's got to be something." I rolled up the old carpet rug. Splinters and dust swirled and I coughed.

Undeterred, I slid my fingers behind the old shelving unit where it had stood against the wall for as long as I could remember.

I peered behind. Black. *A hole.*

"Oh yeah, that's what I need." I tugged harder, listening to the scrape of wood on wood as it slowly moved. China rattled, but I ignored that. Finally, I could thrust my hand inside the small hole. It was round and old. My hand only encountered cobwebs and wood as I fished and hunted. Nothing.

I slid to the floor, the buoyancy that had sustained me over the last hour or so draining away. I chanced a look at the clock and was shocked to find I'd lost three hours.

My stomach rumbled, and I threw a single angry glare at the cupboard and shadowy hole. Hunger was making itself known, so I headed for the kitchen and hunted in the fridge for something to eat.

In the freezer was a dinner I'd prepared, and I threw it into the microwave, touched the buttons and watched it circle around and around on the plate.

The word hidden kept pounding into my brain like a spike. "Where would you hide something, you didn't want anyone else to find?"

I bit my lip, looked out over the garden. My gazed fell on the old outhouse, leaning like a drunken sailor. "The outhouse." The ding of the microwave impinged only slightly as I pushed open the back door, stumbled down the steps and out into the garden. I knew it was an old building. Could it really be that simple?

I hurried through the overgrown plants and visually inspected the building. There could be snakes or anything, my rational brain argued. *True. But if I wanted to hide something, this would be perfect. I mean, the toilet isn't exactly a spot I want to spend time in.* Stood to reason no one else would either.

I pushed on the wood, hearing the creak and groan. Another harder groan sounded, and I stepped back, hoping it wouldn't fall down on me.

After a moment, emboldened by the fact it was still standing, albeit a little less upright, I ventured forward.

This time the push I gave was violent and full of intent. Yes, I needed to get inside, but my gut told me, whatever I was seeking, wasn't going to be in full view.

Crack!

The sound ricocheted like a bullet and I moved, but far too slowly. The structure wobbled and swayed, then lurched in my direction with a thud and smashing sound.

A large splinter of wood sailed through the air and embedded itself in my arm. Deep. Hard. Blood sprayed. "*Oww!*"

I tripped and fell backwards as a large board sprang free and landed on me.

For a moment gray wavered in my vision, then the world turned black.

# CHAPTER 11

*I* groaned, feeling the drag of pain at my senses. The air was cool. I felt distinctly chilled as if the sun had disappeared behind a cloud. "Where am I?" I attempted to raise my arm, but couldn't.

It took all my willpower to open my eyes. Christian loomed above me; his eyes anxious while he spoke carefully. "Don't move. You've hurt yourself badly. There's a large bit of wood in your arm, and you've a nasty black eye and knot on your head." He crouched down beside me.

"What are you doing here?" I was gob smacked with how weak and watery my voice sounded.

"I was worried about you. After you left, I waited a while, hoping you'd calm down enough to listen to me. Then I headed over here. Tabs, I thought you were dead for a moment. You were lying so damned still!" He shook his head. "It was like something or someone told me you needed me. To hurry."

"Just help me up and in—"

"No way. You're going to see the doctor, even if I have to carry you there." His hand shook as he reached for my cheek. "It scared me, Tabs. Please. For me." The cold lump in the middle of my belly, the one I hadn't even known was there before, warmed.

"I... Okay. But first, I need to know if there's something hidden below the floor of the toilet."

Christian gave me an 'are you nuts' look. "You've bumped your head—"

"I'm serious, Christian. She was here. *Alice.* She told me to find what was hidden. I thought inside at first and looked everywhere I could think of. Then when I looked out and saw the outhouse it clicked. Where else would you hide something you didn't want anyone to find? I mean, it's not really somewhere you'd consider as a hiding place for important stuff, is it?"

He opened and closed his mouth. I lay there, waiting for the dull thud in my head to stop.

"Fine." He stood, and I turned my head to watch him. It hurt, but I was determined to see if he found what I was searching for.

He shoved at the pile of wood, all that was left of the structure, and started pushing and heaving until we found the raised floor. "Still with me?"

"Yeah. Not going anywhere," I croaked.

"Fine." His voice was terse.

He kneeled down, and I watched his every movement, the bunching of his shoulders as he shoved up the old wooden planking. He heaved and grunted, the wood splintering at his efforts. "There's nothing... Hang on, what's this?" There was genuine puzzlement in his voice as he scooped something up.

His retreat was slow and careful, and I noted the packet in his hands.

"What is it?"

"I don't know. It's wrapped up and hard." He came closer. "But before we find out what it is, you need to see the doctor."

The pain surged back as my attention was drawn back to it. "Just help me up." I grabbed his hand and tugged, hoping my brain wasn't too rattled. The last thing I needed right now was to drop in a heap at his feet.

The sigh he gave was full of frustration. "Tabs—"

"I'll be fine, but take me to the doctor, if only to put your mind at rest."

*N*ight had fallen by the time he'd deposited me back at his house. "I've got the two of you laid up. At least this way I can keep an eye on you."

The doctor had diagnosed a mild concussion, removed the splinter from my arm and cleaned up the wound site before giving me two stitches, a tetanus jab and prescribed some pain pills. Oh and rest. No exertion. I'd also sprained my ankle. *Bah Humbug!*

My head ached, and I knew Christian would have admitted me to hospital if I'd backed down in the slightest. As it was, the doctor made Christian promise to keep me at home and quiet. And absolutely no driving. That left me stuck here. Of course, he already had Kira and her invalid status to deal with. I didn't want to add to that.

On the lounge opposite me sat Kira, happily engrossed in the tablet device, while I watched Christian puttering around making dinner. My attempt at assistance resisted.

"After dinner, I'd like a look at the package."

As I spoke, Christian took on a sudden stillness and my heart thudded to the pit of my stomach. "You did bring it here, didn't you?"

"Well, yes. But I thought an early night and no stress would be best." I couldn't see his face as he remained turned away, and I wondered what he was thinking and why he thought I wouldn't want to know its contents tonight.

For all of two seconds, I considered how to respond to his words. "It's not stressful, but I need to know what is in it so we can decide what we need to do next."

Christian turned and gifted me with a reproachful look, his forehead creased and mouth flat. "You're meant to be resting."

"And I will. I just need to know what the deal is. That packet contains something that will help us solve the mystery of the

Captain's disappearance. As you pointed out yourself, we're running out of time."

He growled and advanced—two dishes in his hands. He stopped by Kira, waited as she paused her game, then pushed the dish into her hands. The wafting scent of cashew chicken played havoc with my stomach and it burbled noisily.

Kira giggled, the sound cutting through the tension.

Christian handed me the other dish and it looked as tasty as it smelled. "Where's yours?"

"I'm just going to grab it." He hurried back to the kitchen and returned with his dish, took the seat next to me and handed over a fork. "I thought chopsticks might not be such a good idea tonight."

"You don't seriously expect me to think you use—"

"Daddy's fabulous with them. Next time we have Chinese night maybe you could come over."

I couldn't help myself. "Chinese night?"

"We usually have spring rolls, sweet buns, lemon chicken, Mongolian lamb, and sometimes daddy will make Peking Duck!" Kira's rush of words surprised me. "But I don't like his hot and sour soup."

"Wow. Maybe I should come over." I smiled, scooping up some rice. It tasted really good, and for several minutes no one spoke.

Christian grabbed the empty bowls when we were done and I rose to help, only to have him push me back into the seat. "Stay here. I'm just going to throw everything into the dishwasher and get Kira settled in bed. Then we'll take a look."

I seriously didn't want to argue with him. My head hurt, thumping enough that all I wanted was peace and quiet, so after wishing Kira goodnight I settled back and waited until he was done.

The sound of the wind blowing through the trees outside, combined the cool air lulled me, and I was drifting when Christian returned. "We can do this tomorrow."

He scooped me up, and I had to give in and agree I wasn't up to arguing. "I'm sorry."

"What for?" I felt the rumble of his words and an answering tremor surged through me.

"Because I couldn't stay awake." Coward, I told myself. Time to tell the truth—the whole unvarnished truth. "Because I couldn't allow myself to need you and your assistance."

Down the hallway he padded, with me caught up against his chest. "Don't worry about it."

But I did. Because I couldn't give up my control, I scared him and got hurt. Caused him more hassles when all he'd wanted was... what, exactly? But there wasn't an answer for my question. Instead Christian laid me carefully on the bed, as if I were spun silk.

He started to tug at my clothes, and I noted it was his bedroom. The scene of last night's passion laden adventures. "Christian—"

"*Shhhh.*" He continued while I gave in. Once I was in my pajamas, he settled me in the bed. "I'll be back in a minute."

I rolled over and snuggled down. My eyes heavy.

If he returned that quickly, I didn't know, because Morpheus already held me in his arms.

# CHAPTER 12

The night passed slowly.

Several times Christian woke me, offered water and proceeded through the litany of questions the doctor had insisted he ask.

When the morning came, it brought dreary gray skies and a light drizzle. I woke to a reminder of the urgent requirements of nature, and returned to the bed, where I settled in feeling a most unusual sense of well-being. The kind I hadn't felt since long before my father died. Christian entered the room, bearing a cup of tea and some toast. I tried to rise, but he ushered me back against the pillows, then with quick steps settled on the bed beside me.

"How's Kira?"

Christian smiled. "Gone to Peta's."

"What?" I reached for my watch where Christian had placed it the night before and gasped with dismay when I read the time. Ten a.m.. "No! I've never slept that late before!"

He grinned. "You obviously needed it. Besides, I needed to be able to talk to you about the package. It's always easier to do it without little ears around. And we need to talk about what we're going to do... About us."

I colored at his words. *Us.* I wasn't sure I was ready to even consider that.

I must have squirmed because the smile he granted me was soft and knowing.

"Look, I'm not sure—"

Christian reached for the tray and placed it on the floor on his side of the bed. When he turned back to me, I couldn't mistake the intensity in his expression. "I know. I understand. But I don't have sex with women I don't have feelings for. Strong feelings, Tabs. I want to see this through. What we have, it feels good and right. It feels..." He raked his hands through his hair. "And therein lies the rub. I feel, Tabs."

His words went a long way towards soothing my disquiet, because deep down, I wanted to acknowledge that I too felt.

I bit my lip, trying to hold back the flood of emotions and words that would betray me, but the stare he pinned me with was questioning. "I... I don't know what I feel. It's... complicated."

He roared with laughter at that, and I wanted to hit him, because these feelings scared me. Couldn't he see that?

When he subsided, he slid his arms around me and pulled me close. "Tabs, I'll take that, because I'm a patient man. Well, normally." Now he popped a kiss on my forehead.

"I..." I wanted to thank him or yell at him for pushing. I wanted to kiss him. So many wild feelings warred inside me. I stopped, because I desperately needed time to come to terms with his words and needed to change the subject. "Where's the package?"

He turned to the bedside table, rattled in the cupboard and slid back against the pillows, gripping it. "Want to open it?"

*Do I ever.*

The covering was some kind of leather, but it was dry and brittle under my hands. I eased the folds open and to reveal a further, smaller packet. The paper mottled with age, the old wax broken and melted across the parchment.

With great care, I pulled it free with a tiny hissing scrape.

"Should I open it?"

From his pocket, Christian removed a pair of cotton gloves. "Let me."

I handed it over, my stomach flopping and lurching.

Christian turned over the packet, eying it here and there before laying it on the bed and carefully unfolding the letter. He squinted. "Holy hell!"

"What?" I leaned forward, hoping to make out the words.

*My dearest Alice,*

*By the time you receive this missive, I shall be on my way to you. The latest mission was protracted, but I've finally fulfilled my duty to Her Majesty. Should I fail to return, you should know that the crown will hold the property on which we so briefly lived, in perpetuity, for our family and descendants. You shall never have to fear the loss of your home again.*

*I am enclosing a key. This fits a drawer hidden in the back of the escritoire. It contains details of my missions, for they were all tied to the one outcome. Should I fail, ensure no one can access these records.*

*There are others, and they are dangerous, so you should be prepared and aware at all times. My opponents will seek to undermine my work. They will attempt to find what I've secreted away in my service to Queen and country. Those that would defeat me are great in number, my love.*

*What they seek is precious, though. Should they find what they seek, they will be undefeatable.*

*Once more, I count the days until we are together again, but should I not return, know that you are forever in my heart and soul.*

*I Remain,*

*Yours Affectionately...*

I sat, stunned by the contents of the letter. He'd known there was a chance he wouldn't return and had taken great pains to reassure her.

"Does it say anywhere where he was when he sent it?"

Christian turned over the letter, checking the back before he shook his head. "No. But I think of greater import is, where is the key he spoke of?"

Then it twigged. "Hang on. The day you came to visit, after Kira's accident. I found a key in a box. It was tied to a blue ribbon. Could that be it?"

Christian's smile was wide and beguiling. "It could just be what we're looking for. Where did you say you put it?"

I frowned. "In the box, in the kitchen. It's in full view—"

He rose. "We should go check it out then."

I lurched up, my knees a little wobbly, but at least my head was on straight.

## CHAPTER 13

The house was waiting for me when we got back there. It felt as if it was welcoming us home. Strange, while I'd always felt an affinity to this place, it felt and seemed like so much more now.

We clattered up the steps, and I stopped, my hand on the handle of the screened door as I caught sight of a yellow page stuck between the jamb and wood edge of the door.

I reached carefully and realized it was crinkled, as if caught there. I stepped back.

"What's wrong?"

Christian's voice echoed through my mind as I strove to understand the ramifications of what I was seeing.

"Someone's been here. *Inside.*"

He shoved me aside and behind him, shielding me, and peered down. "Where's your house key?"

I held it out and he snatched it up, reaching into his pocket for a handkerchief and opened the door with great care.

"What... What are you doing?" I couldn't believe he'd just barge in, but that's exactly what he did.

"Keep an eye out."

He advanced slowly, and I kept my gaze on him. Watching his

cautious movements. On the floor lay strewn the results of years of gathering. Teacups smashed and photos face down, the backs hacked at.

When he returned from the kitchen, strain bracketed his mouth with white lines. "Find the research and the key. Then we call the police."

I frowned but gave a nod. In television shows, they never just marched in like this. I opened my mouth, but he laid a soft finger against my lips.

"We need to find the information and key, then let them do their job. If they get wind of the research, they're going to want to see it. That could cause more issues, slow down our ability to act. We don't have that luxury."

The argument I'd been formulating in my mind, dried up like water in the desert. He was right, of course.

I hurried to the kitchen. The box remained where I'd left it, old gowns lying half in and half out, the battered feather on top of the bottom gown, just as I'd left it. "It should be in here." I fished around underneath the heavy material until I felt the outline of the old cardboard. I shuffled and dug, before eventually pulling it up. My heart thud madly in my chest as I opened it... Inside lay the key, the faded blue ribbon hiding it. I exhaled and slumped. "Thank God."

"Okay. Find the letters, then we'll get them hidden in the car and make the call."

A flash of intuition had me grabbing the old material and lifting it over my head. Christian quirked an eyebrow at my action but said nothing.

The old metal warmed against my skin as I scurried around, hunting for the letters and journals. I found them in my underwear drawer in the bedroom, exactly where I'd left them. Yet for all they were in the same place, they'd been unwrapped, inspected and read.

I felt violated and deeply concerned with what had happened. "Christian, I can't believe someone would come in here and help themselves to the letters." My voice rose, strident and uncertain.

His face, though, was implacable. "At least it was only the letters and you weren't here." A tic had begun pulsing at the side of his jaw, and I felt a moment of fear.

"What do you mean?"

"If you'd been here, alone. It would have been worse." When he gazed at me, I read the fear and fury he couldn't hide.

The look on his face married with the sudden lurch in my stomach. "Oh my God!"

"Exactly."

Suddenly I felt nauseated. Too much was happening, and a lot of it wasn't a positive experience. I reached out blindly, but he caught me close. "I won't let anything happen to you. I..." He stopped, as if unable to form a coherent sentence. The expansion of his chest and the sudden stillness caught my attention and I looked up from his chest, where I'd tucked my head.

He was staring over my shoulder. I followed his look and inhaled sharply. Before us stood the Captain.

*The room melted away to a fluffy gray fog. I felt the bite of Christian's touch, though. He'd never seen the captain before, I guessed.*

*"You're the one from my Alice's line?"*

*I felt Christian's convulsive nod.*

*"He is, Captain. He helped me to find the letter and the key, but someone was here. They were searching."*

*"Yes. I saw them. A man and a woman. I knew their faces—"*

*"You know who they were?" Christian bit the words out and I grabbed his hand, hoping he'd hold on to what I suspected was a seriously stretched temper.*

*"I don't know their names, but I knew their ancestor. The one who sent them to look for the key. She and hers are dangerous. They will lie, kill, steal in order to gain access to this place."*

*His words echoed.* This house. This house was the thing they wanted most of all, *I knew in an instant. Yet the question was why. "Why here? What is special about this property?"*

*"You are a clever young lady. I can't tell you everything, only that the key is indeed important and your assumption that this place is integral is part of the answer."*

*Frustration scored me. Never a straight answer.*

*The Captain's smile died a little, becoming a tight frown. "I cannot answer these direct questions. I can only offer guidance. You found the letter. You found the key. Now you must find the journals and orders I hid. They will show you what you must know to win the day and reunite Alice and I."*

*"Why? Why must they resume the property? Captain, we don't understand—" Christian's urgent tones were cut off by the Captain raising his hand.*

*"I cannot give you that information. In life, I only came to understand my part. What I knew in life is all I can share."*

*The Captain turned, and for the first time, I felt his loneliness and pain like a weight on my soul. "Captain, I'm trying."*

*He turned his head, glancing over his shoulder to me. "I know."*

*Then he was gone.*

"*H*e's a mountain of a man, just like the way you describe him. How the hell do you deal with his cryptic answers, though?"

I shook my head at his words. We'd just arrived back at Christian's after the whole nine yards of police carry on, and my energy levels had been flagging with Pete turning up moments later. "I just do what I need to do."

I rubbed at the abraded skin around my neck. The material, dust encrusted and harsh, had irritated and as soon as we'd got inside I'd whipped off the material from where I'd hidden it beneath my top.

A swipe of calamine had taken the edge off the itchiness, but the burn remained. Christian entered the lounge carrying a coffee for me and a cup of tea for Peta, who'd perched on the other armchair. He disappeared back into the kitchen to return only a moment later carrying his own mug, then settled on the arm of my chair.

Peta watched him, her eyes gleaming. "Ah, so it's like that, is it?"

She winked broadly, and I felt the burn of a deep blush, while Christian chuckled.

"A gentleman never tells."

"Oh God! That's so funny! You're no gentleman, but you don't need to tell me anything more. I can read body language. Remember, I work for the government."

"*Local* Government," reproved Christian and she sniggered again.

"Anyway, back to the matter at hand. What's your next step?"

I frowned at Peta's question.

"The escritoire was missing from the house, and I didn't have a clue as to where to find it. I mean, it's not in the house and—"

"Wait." Peta raised her hand. "Desk?"

"Yes, that's what an escritoire is. A desk." I leaned forward. "You have that funny look on your face."

"Oh well, you would too. See, there's this family furniture. Mom was given it, and some came to me and other bits were meant for—"

"The desk is mine. I'd forgotten all about it. Is it still in your garage?" Christian raised his hand until it lay on my shoulder, curving and deliciously warm.

"Sure and it is, brother of mine." Peta chuckled at her faux Irish accent, and Christian merely rolled his eyes.

"So, all this time, we've both been sitting on the answers, yet neither of us had any clue." I shook my head. "But didn't your wife...?"

Christian started rubbing my shoulder, slowly and in a most intoxicating manner. "Janet isn't into antiques or old stuff."

I blinked, trying to clear the sensual haze that was settling on my brain from his movements. After all, Peta was here and my coffee... *Splosh!* "Ouch!"

Christian moved like lightning, grabbing the mug from my hand. "Come on, I'll run cold water."

He marched me to the kitchen, turned on the faucet and shoved my hand under. The burn swelled, then faded a little. I felt embarrassed. "I'm not usually so clumsy"

*N*ot long after I burned myself, Peta decided it was time to head home. "After all, Liam had Kira all afternoon to himself, while I came a-visiting. But since she's staying tonight, he has to go home, and I'd like to feed him before he leaves." She'd hustled out the door while I nursed my sore hand. At least my head was feeling rather normal again.

The door shut with a thud behind her.

"We should think about dinner. Any preferences?" Christian walked over to the fridge and opened the door. "I have some chicken, some fish or steak. Take your pick."

I couldn't pick and shook my head. "Your house, you choose." I decided the easy way out was an option tonight. So, he grabbed the large meat container, extract two pieces of beef and pop them on the grill of his gas stovetop.

"Salad okay?"

"Sounds fantastic. What do you want me to do?" I half rose.

"No way. You're injured. Sit down and we can talk. Wine?" He held up a bottle of something wet and white contained in a green bottle.

We'd face a long and difficult day, so there could only be one answer. "Oh yeah!"

He laughed at my response and hunted in the cupboard beside the fridge, then emerged with two glasses.

As Christian set about cooking, I sipped my wine. "So next step is visiting Peta's and find this desk. Open the secret drawer... Did you even know it existed?"

"I didn't have a clue. After Mom and Dad moved to the island, a lot of furniture got stored. I mean, I knew there was a desk, but I didn't really pay that much attention to it. It was in my parents' house and was part of the inheritance deal. Of course, Janet and I were married when they moved and Peta lived in the house on the island, so it wasn't an issue to leave it in the garage."

I bit my lip at his words. "You lived here with Janet?" My stomach kind of flip-flopped at the idea that he'd shared the same bed with her in the room where we'd—I shied away from the thought of had sex.

"No. We lived in the supervisor's house on the water, but we were only there for a couple of months before she upped and offed. I bought this after. She never lived here, Tabs. Only Kira and I."

I felt so damned stupid and shallow, but it rankled that she might have tainted this place where we were growing our connection.

As if he could read my thoughts, he put down the tongs and stalked over to me. "I promise, what we have means so much more than what Janet and I shared. I wouldn't cheapen it by—"

"I know that. It just feels icky is all." I couldn't think of a better description but the feel of him enfolding me in his arms soothed those worries. Chased them away until they were little more than receding shadows.

He bent down as I raised my head, and we kissed. Light and warmth flooded me again, and the sense of well-being I associated with Christian rippled through my body.

With a shaky laugh, I pulled away. "Okay, the desk. You didn't know about the drawer I assume?"

He returned to the grill. "No. There was never anything about it that seemed more than I saw." For a moment, the only sound in the kitchen was the sizzle of the meat.

"Okay then. So, it's in Peta's garage. We can check that in the morning, but that means we're stuck tonight. Nothing more to do."

The grin he shot at me was super-hot and cheeky and I gulped my wine, spluttered and blushed.

He laughed and came over, patted my back and I felt darned foolish I couldn't even *look* at him!

"I can think of lots to do. Including kissing you."

A peck on the side of my face had me rolling my eyes. "You've got to be kidding me."

His hands found my shoulders and squeezed and just like that the nerves under my skin took up their wild ululations of joy, my center melted, and arousal spiked. When he gently reached for my chin and angled it up, my lips were already parted and ready for him.

He moved closer, between my legs and tugged me up so my body dragged against his, the feel of his arousal burned through my clothing. The clinch turned wild, lips dragging, tongues tangling, and oxygen deprivation was the only thing that pulled me back to sanity.

"Christian..." I sucked in a deep breath and a tangy, scorching scent filled the air. "That was hot enough to—"

"Dinner!" He pulled away and scrambled back to the kitchen. A burbling laugh tripped off my lips.

"At least I'm not the only one who loses concentration."

He grunted and set to saving our food.

By the time the table was set, and the plates loaded, my emotional equilibrium had been regained—somewhat. We ate in near silence, with only the odd comment or question. The rattle of cutlery on the plates acted as an aphrodisiac. I shivered with the intensity of my hunger—and I didn't hunger for food.

By unspoken agreement, we abandoned the meal halfway through. All it took was a heated glance and the crook of his finger and I followed him, wineglass in hand, to the bedroom.

Once there, I took a deep draught, the headiness of what I was agreeing to intoxicating my senses.

"I want you, Tabitha. But I want you without any magic. Without any outside factors. *I want you.* Stay with me tonight? Let me love you?"

The intensity of his gaze couldn't compare to the emotional response his words pulled from me. The riot of heat and hunger that zinged and raced across nerves.

Now it was my turn to answer, and I needed a moment or two. I took another sip. Inhaled deeply. Procrastinating? *Yes. Absolutely.* Sure of myself? *Not at all!*

"I'm not the kind of girl who—"

"Sleeps around. I understand that. But whatever is going on between us is more than just a fling, isn't it?"

My stomach wobbled. "I... Yes." There, I'd said it. Agreed that there was more at stake than a simple—and that word didn't even begin to describe how I felt—sexual encounter.

With great care, I popped my wine down onto the bedside table, then reached up and tugged at the first button of my blouse. Then I slid my hand down the placket and opened the next, while capturing his gaze. His face reddened and his Adam's Apple bobbed up and down and I couldn't contain the grin on my face. Oh yes, he was as affected by the situation as I was.

I didn't stop to wonder or ask, just continued my slow release of fasteners. Pop, pop, pop!

Once the last blouse button gave, I reached upwards and slid the soft cotton from my shoulders. A whisper of wind slid over my skin. My nipples puckered and I shivered. It broke the magic connection between us, enough that I could step back, suck in a breath and clear my mind, just a little.

Christian advanced. A step. Then another. Every bit closer and that small amount of sanity I regained fled until he touched me. Then the last vestige fizzled away.

He framed my face, the touch feather light, and as he drew closer, I prepared myself for the onslaught of passion, while my body burned with hunger.

"Christian." I heard the moan and knew, dimly, it was me making that otherworldly sound. Then we kissed.

Lightning flashed and desire exploded while the last emotional barrier keeping us apart fell away.

Now came the tug of clothing, stripping each other of the layers that kept our bodies apart.

My bra melted and his pants gaped as I wrestled with his belt.

Blind.

Desperate.

Finally, we were skin to skin. Electricity arced everywhere we touched, and we shuffled—a mad dance of carnality—toward the bed.

We fell.

Tangled.

"More." I couldn't resist demanding everything and he answered with a wickedly sinful gasp.

"Whatever my lady desires."

Desire I did.

My belly hollowed as he skimmed his lips across my collarbone, stopping for an instant at one peaked nipple before working his way down my belly. He gave a swipe across my flesh with his tongue, darting into the indent before continuing.

I writhed, needing more, while my insides melted with every quivering, passionate movement.

"Christian!" *Oh God!* My body was on fire, my focus narrowed on the single point of pleasure that he worked. When his fingers and tongue met at my center, I screamed and arched. Every fiber of my being lost in the orgasm that clashed through me.

"Not enough." He spoke, and the rumble of his words, the whispery breath scorched me.

I tangled my fingers in the sheets. I wanted to touch him. I wanted him inside me. I wanted it. *Now!*

"Please!" I reached for his shoulders and pulled, tugged. Whatever it took to demand the fulfilment my body craved.

Now there were no drugging kisses as he moved. Power and speed met in equal portions until he loomed.

"Christian, I want you."

He gazed at me. The look deep and yet drugging. "Condom."

He fished around under the pillow and dragged out a foil packet.

I must have given a flash of understanding and dismay at the same time, because he grinned. "Here, you do the honors." He slid the packet between my nerveless fingers and once again, the flash of sanity returned.

I tore at the packet, sliding the latex from within the pack and made quick work of its application.

He was huge. Engorged and ready. Yet I wanted him, not the slide of the protective cover.

"Tabs?" He spoke, and it broke my introspection.

I reached up, cupped his head and dragged it back down for a drugging kiss that catapulted me back into the maelstrom.

His hands found my breasts, firmed them, and stroked my nipples while he nudged my legs apart again. The rasp of hair against my damp swollen folds intoxicated me again, and I let myself fall into the abyss.

When he surged, his cock fully embedded within my body, it felt like coming home. Every move, every rock ratcheted the insatiable need to new heights.

The orgasm climbed, swirled, then smashed down on me, suffocating and filling until there was no him and me. Just us. Two lovers in a world no one else could breach.

Together we clung while our bodies took over. Then the sensation and urgency faded away, leaving me exhausted and lost.

"Tabs?" Christian's voice was as raspy as I'm sure mine would be.

"Yeah."

"I think I love you."

CHAPTER 14

*M*orning came around and the discomfort I felt from the night before, from Christian's sort of declaration, hadn't lifted. It wasn't that it didn't make me feel good; it was just that I wasn't really ready to consider anything more than a transitory relationship. Besides, I wondered if he, too, was worried that some of the feelings that we were dealing with weren't echoes of the Captain and Alice's desire to be together.

Instead, I kept up a steady stream of chatter, keeping everything light. "That cup of coffee was just what I needed, thanks Christian. When do you want to head over to Peta's?"

His eyes narrowed. "Once I've washed up, we can head over."

I nodded and avoided his gaze. Yes, he'd already questioned how I felt over breakfast and I'd hedged. He'd been hurt. The way his lips tightened was just a clue to his emotional state.

Normally, I would have offered to assist, but today I escaped to the bathroom, brushed my teeth and hair and wasted time until he called. When I emerged he captured my hand. "We need to talk about last night, again. Tabitha, I understand my words frightened you but—"

Unable to escape the conversation, I took a moment. Carefully examined my feelings because I couldn't lie or prevaricate. The declaration demanding nothing less than honesty. "No. You didn't scare me, Christian. I'm just not ready to talk about it. I need time to think. We both do. After all, this whole situation is strange and feels almost..." I fished about for the right term, one that wouldn't offend, but the best I could come up with, was, "*voyeuristic*."

"Dammit, Tabitha, don't write it off as—"

I cut him off with a wave of my hand. "I'm not. But let's be realistic for a moment. What if what this is, isn't about us, but the Captain and Alice? What if this is some kind of damned imitation or resonance from them? If this is more, then we deserve to know for sure. Not to be guessing at it."

His face took on a ruddy glow. "It's not—"

"How can you be *sure*, Christian? Is it like last time, with Janet?"

He flinched, and I wanted to swallow those last words. Make them unsaid. But now there was no chance. He straightened up, stiff and remote in those seconds. "You're right, of course. Let's go." Christian turned and walked away, leaving me regretting everything I'd blurted out in my frustration.

"Christian?" I hurried after him, but he shook his head and ushered me out the door.

The drive to Peta's house was fraught. Horribly uncomfortable, and neither of us were willing to give in. I might have hurt him infinitesimally at breakfast, but now it felt like a bloody great chasm existed between us.

On arrival he slid out of the car, opened my door for me but didn't speak. I murmured my "thank you," but he didn't smile.

Peta must have read the distance between us, and I wanted to cry. I'd alienated the only man I'd had any desire to consider a long-term relationship with, and his sister was hungry for information.

"What's happened?" Her gaze whipped from Christian to me and back again.

Christian shook his head. "Let's go find this damned drawer." The look Peta shot at me told me I'd be answering questions, privately, before too long. I trailed behind the two of them, wondering where Kira could be. I didn't ask though. I felt like I didn't have that right.

The knowledge that I'd stuffed everything up left me aching. In the past, when people had mentioned broken hearts and the whole physical pain thing, I'd scoffed. Now, I knew what they meant and it ached. A whole damn lot.

I rubbed my chest, hoping no one would notice my action, but I should have known better. The glance that Peta shot my way was full of sympathy and understanding.

"I cleared the space around the desk, so you can get in. Oh, and Liam took Kira so you could search in peace. I thought that might help."

Christian grunted, and I sighed. "Thanks, Peta."

We advanced, and I let Christian take the lead, his fingers sliding over the escritoire, tugging gently on the scrollwork and pushing the drawers in before pulling them out.

It took ages, and we still hadn't found the lock when I stepped forward. "Do you mind if I try?"

"I can't find it, but maybe you can." His words speared me, because I knew that wasn't all he'd wanted to say. He stepped aside and I fished a small torch from my bag and let the beam of illumination play over the woodwork. I searched for joins and was about to give up, when something glittered at the very bottom, down by the leg. I hunkered down and felt the edges. *There!*

The key in my pocket almost burned, as if it knew it was once again going to become one with its lock. I slid it into the opening and listened as it grated. Then the drawer, hidden below the work surface of the desk, dropped free. A bundle of pages bounced as the wood hit the floor with a thud.

*A*fter finding the cache, we'd retreated back to Christian's. The tension still cut through me, but there was an air of expectation too. Just when I had hope that we might overcome some part of my mess, we entered the house to find the Captain, waiting there for us.

*The room held a darkness I'd not noticed before. "Captain? What's wrong?"*

*"Time grows short now. The others, those who work against us, are growing stronger. Soon, we will not be able to defeat them. You need to release us so we can complete our task. Otherwise the echoes of purgatory will spill over into your reality."*

*"Purgatory?"*

*"Where we exist, my dear. Tell me, Christian. Have you found what you seek?"*

*Christian nodded and held up the sheaf of papers. The ones we'd decided we would examine once we arrived back here.*

*"You have found my orders. Excellent." The smile on his face faded when he noted the drawn looks of ours. He glanced from side to side. "What's wrong?"*

*"Nothing." I gave a shrug, but he advanced, the glow of joy fading away so his appearance took on an almost transparent quality. This was some-thing I'd need to consider later.*

*"Child, anything that worries you, can impact on this situation." Every word thudded into my brain.*

*Before I could open my mouth, Christian wrapped his arms around me. "She thinks that the situation with us is controlled by you. Your emotions and needs. Could she be right?" He spoke coldly, yet the warmth of his touch bled into me, and the heat I'd been missing since our argument finally returned.*

*"Ah. As to that, I cannot answer. Clearly whatever has passed pains you both, but I am a mere ghost." He spread his hands expansively, and the corner of his lips arced downwards. "Little more than a memory of the past. I remember love, but now, the only emotions that control me are concern for my Alice and the need to be reunited and to complete my final mission. I would do what I could—"*

*"We understand, Captain. We're planning to going through the papers so we can backtrack, but if you can give us—"*

*"I cannot tell you where to look, but the answer lies within the sheets. Read them well. It is hidden, but those who seek will find the truth." His*

*emphasis seemed to tire him because he faded further, so we could barely see him.*

*"We'll find you. Reunite you. We're working as fast as we can."*

*"I know, my dear. However, time grows short and that which is contained within the home cannot be overstated." On those words, he disappeared from view.*

I tottered to the table, surprised at just how much that short interlude had cost in terms of energy. "Tabitha?" Christian spoke quietly as he hunkered down beside me. "Are you alright?"

"I honestly don't know. Each and every visit seems to drain me more. This one though more than ever before. I don't understand why." I shrugged and reached for the papers, but Christian stilled my action, sliding his hand over mine, then gripping lightly.

"I'm sorry, Tabitha. I didn't want to accept that what you said was right." His hand shook where it hovered above mine.

"I know. It's okay. We'll get through this, then talk about it. Just don't..." I swallowed, nervous that he'd brush off my words, "don't leave me."

He dropped a kiss on my forehead. "I won't. Now, I'll grab us both a cold drink while you get the letters into order and we can begin."

"I'm grateful Peta is keeping Kira."

"She's a great sister. Plus, I think she knew that we needed time and space. Parenting doesn't come with a manual, and she's forever telling me that this way she can make mistakes and hand Kira back when it gets too hard. Preparation, according to her, for when her own finally make an appearance."

I laughed at his words; thankful we'd settled into a routine reminiscent of what we'd had before my stupid comments.

I rose, and he pushed me back into the seat. "What do you want, and I'll get it?"

"My notebook. That way we can sit down and sift through the

information. I like to be able to write it out. It helps me to sort out the information."

Christian returned quickly with the small box I had all the letters, my notebook and where I'd decided to stash the key.

The whistle of the kettle drew him into the kitchen, and I took a moment to compose myself before checking the dates on the large parchment piles. I settled them into date order and was just about to start reading the first when Christian returned with our coffees.

"There's a bit of reading to get through." He took the seat opposite me at the table and spread his hands to encompass all the information we had to read through.

"There is, but there was something about the way the Captain spoke that leads me to believe the answer is here, somewhere." I reached out, gathered up the first page and looked at Christian. "You look through the next one. If the two of us are working our way through, hopefully we'll find the clues sooner."

I shoved the next one at him and settled in. As I read, I wrote notes in the booklet, but by the end, nothing jumped out at me. I glanced at Christian. The light shone through the window, his hair appeared haloed. He was a good man. One who wanted to bring me pleasure. One who professed he *thought* he loved me. He cared deeply enough to be hurt by my comments.

He loved Kira and would do anything for her, even down to putting up with Janet, the ex-wife who only ever seemed to want to spoil what he had. So what was holding me back? I could tell myself it was purely because I didn't want to run the risk that it all centered on the needs of Alice and her Captain.

"What are you thinking about?" Christian held out his hand and on impulse I grasped it, grateful for the warmth.

"Us. Why I'm so unsure. What I want."

His eyes glowed. "What do you want, Tabitha?"

"You. Us. Everything I'm feeling for you to be real and mine. Ours."

He smiled. As far as declarations went it wasn't a lot, but I fancied he knew that for me, like was reminiscent of stepping into the unknown, let alone the fact I'd said it out loud.

"Once and for all, let me say, that my comments last night weren't meant to scare you. I'm unsure after Janet and I understand your fears, but inside me." He thumped his chest." There's this well that deepens every time I look at you. I feel warmth and a need to be with you. Emotions I thought I understood are changing. Becoming more." He gripped his hair, as if trying to pinpoint exactly what his emotions were was impossible. I wanted to reach out, but when I moved, he shook his head. "I'm not much good at smooth talk, but you need to know what I feel."

In that moment, I did. Or at least, thought I did. Confusion rolled again. Each time I was sure, it melted away like frost under the morning sun.

"Christian, I want to reciprocate. Say I feel the same, but I'm afraid and I honestly don't know. You promised me time and much as I want to say yes, right now all I can say is maybe, until I know." Tears burned my eyes, because I felt desperately helpless.

He touched my cheek with soft fingertips. "I understand. All this is intense and with so many competing issues, it's hard to find a point at which it becomes easy to understand."

I turned away, because right now, it was too much to cope with and as if he understood; he sat back with a sigh. I spun around and saw him rubbing his hand across his eyes. "Maybe what we need is a break?"

I saw the tired smile on his face. "Much as I'd like to, I think we need to finish this as quickly as we can."

I picked up the letter and paraphrased what I thought were the important parts into the notebook.

Then Christian did the same.

Nothing stood out for either of us, and we moved to the next missives and continued the sequence. It must have been about the sixth letter, as our stomachs growled, that we stopped. "This feels useless." Dejection fluttered, and I slid the letter onto the discard pile.

"We're hungry and tired. I'll rustle something up in the kitchen and you see if you can find anything in the next one." I nodded, grateful we'd soon be taking a break, yet when I lifted the sheet, I knew I'd found the one containing what we needed. Excitement skittered along nerve endings.

"Christian? I think I've found something! Quick, come here." I rose and hurried to the kitchen. "Let me read this bit out to you.

*"Once you are in receipt of the package, you must then travel to St Paul's Cathedral. There, the priest on duty will grant you holy water in a vial, and a small lead casket in which you must place the package for the journey. The priest will bless it and you, giving you the best chance of completing this mission.*

*The casket must not leave your possession. Carry it with you to the wharf, then secrete it within your cabin. Under no circumstances should you open it. To do so will negate all we've worked to achieve. When you reach your home, ensure a priest undertakes the blessing of your foundations. Find a place, well hidden in or within the foundations of your home—the Colonial Office has undertaken the necessary preparations, ensuring it will not pass out of the ownership of your family, as we've discussed. The water you will receive is from the river Jordan, and we believe it will protect your family. Sprinkle it below and above the item, though you have already declared that the foundations of your home were blessed. Somewhere within would be the most efficacious position for this item.*

*All care must be taken to ensure the success of this mission. Failure will result in evil such as we are unable to match.*

*Take all care, my friend.*

"Are we in over our head?" I glanced up at Christian, who seemed as stunned as I was.

"I honestly don't know. But what we need to do next is find out where the Captain is buried then try to sort out the location of the package. And maybe find a priest."

## CHAPTER 15

We hurried to the house and just stood there. I bit my nail as I visually scoured the rocks that formed the base of the house. Nothing stood out or seemed unusual. It just looked...the same. I sighed and moved to the next side, but nothing felt different.

"This is useless." I swiped my hand across my face. The tiredness that dogged me, and the lack of information dragged at my mind. Disheartened best described my mood right now as I plopped onto the grass.

Christian frowned, then slumped down beside me. "I agree. We don't know what we should do next. It seems like we figure out one problem then face another." He looked as defeated, with slumped shoulders and ruffled hair, as I felt.

"I think we need help, but what kind, I don't know." I stared at the rocks, tracing the old dried mortar with my gaze. The gray mass was broken down, with bits crumbling and breaking away here and there.

As a child, I'd played here, dragging my fingers along the uneven lines and digging at it, until my father came out, stumping down the steps and bellowing at me to leave it alone. The memory warmed me. "I remember digging at the mortar. My dad, he'd get cranky and come out, then as punishment, he'd make me help with the housework. Stuff I hated like folding the washing or cleaning the toilet."

"Sounds like your Dad was a great one."

I scooted closer and Christian tugged me close. "He was. We were so close. Losing him hurt so much. He was all I had. My mother left when I was young. She didn't want the responsibility or the lifestyle. It cramped her."

"Just like Janet."

I frowned. It was odd and more than a little to consider that his wife had been so like my mother. "What's the odds?"

"What?"

"See, doesn't it strike you as odd that my mother and your wife were so similar? I mean, what if..." I shook my head and pushed away the fanciful thought. As if there was more to it than that.

"What if what, Tabs?" He pushed, and I pushed up from the ground, refusing to give words to my thoughts.

"Nothing. Come on. Let's see what we can find out." I hurried into the house, through the lounge and into the kitchen, deciding the best bet was to contact the local priest. He, after all, might have someone to contact. I sat down in a seat and tugged out my phone.

Before I could dial though, I stopped. Slumped in my chair as I realized, I didn't have a phone number and what was I going to say? *'Hi, a ghost gave me the job of finding and dealing with a religious artefact. But he's been dead over a hundred years and I don't actually know what I'm looking for.'* Oh, wouldn't that be a scream? They'd lock me up. Hell, I'd lock myself up for that!

"Tabitha? Tell me what's wrong."

The dam burst as anger and frustration slammed into me. "Dammit, think Christian. I'm going to ring a priest, ask him to come around and help me inspect my house while looking for something which I don't even know for sure is still here. When he asks me how I know it's here, I'll tell him a ghost showed me how to find some letters and he'll believe me. Because why? Because he's a priest? Because he thinks I'm telling the truth?" I thrust my hands into the air.

"When you put it like that it does sound fantastical, but I had a thought of someone we could call."

I stopped. "You know someone?"

"My old professor. He knew a lot of people and might be able to give us a hand."

I grimaced. "And of course, he'll believe you." Of course he would. Right before we both got sectioned and sent to the nearest mental health facility, I thought sourly.

"In my profession, we follow many leads, know many people, because information comes from a variety of sources. We don't discount them as easily as you might think."

"But you didn't think of him before?" I wanted to swallow the words as soon as I'd finished.

"No. Because we didn't have enough to go forward with at the time."

Now I stared at him, swallowing the unspoken threat. *Because he'd question our sanity.*

I waited, sure he'd add what I thought, but after a couple of moments I huffed, got up and filled the kettle, refusing to listen to Christian.

After an eternity, piping hot coffees prepared I felt his touch and turned my head. "So?"

"He's going to join us tomorrow. It piqued his interest."

The long day stretched out as we scoured the footings of the house, poking at the rocks and bricks, but nothing broke free. We didn't find anything untoward either. I really didn't expect it to. At the back of the property there was an access hole. I stared at the dark maw as Christian stuffed his shirt into his pants, tightened his belt. I handed him the torch.

"You're sure there're no snakes under there?" The beat of my heart was both rapid and suffocating. I might be deathly afraid of them, but my fear that he'd get hurt overcame all my previous fears.

"Nope. But if there's any, I clobber them with a rock," His chortle didn't lift my mood. "Look, if the item is in the brickwork, I'll see it then skedaddle straight out. Now hand me the broom."

I did, while numbness overtook me. He got down on the ground and wriggled and squirmed inside the small space until only his feet remained in view. Then they too disappeared. I heard an odd banging thud and waited, sure the building was about to collapse on him, or some reptilian creature would bite. I didn't even want to think of the eight-legged critters under there.

"Christian?"

"All good." His muffled words didn't alleviate the disquiet that burgeoned. The occasional oomph fed my fears and long moments passed. Then I heard a crunch and, "Oww!"

"Christian?" I crept closer to the manhole.

"Yeah. You'll never believe what I've found. Another trunk and— hang on!" His voice took on an excited tone. More echoes sounded, followed by a scraping sound, which came nearer and nearer. At the mouth of the access an old wood sea trunk emerged, and I hunkered down, found the old metal handles and tugged. I pushed it away, more concerned that Christian would emerge healthy and whole.

His dusty and cobwebbed head emerged as he crawled out of the small area. I hunkered down and extended my hand. "Here, let me help."

"That should be my line." His grin warmed me. He slapped the mess off and stood. "I suggest we pack this up and head for home."

"But why?"

He shook his head and fussed with a pocket before tugging me close. "I found it, so I guess we should celebrate."

For a moment his words didn't even make a difference, then I started. "Celebrate?"

"Yes, but let's get all this into the car, then head home."

I tugged at the heavy wooden box, dragging it away so he could grab the other handle. Then we hefted it towards the car. Into the boot we manhandled it, the door shut as I noticed the plume from an oncoming vehicle. I shaded my eyes and couldn't miss the tension that suddenly had Christian stiff beside me. He slid his hand around my waist. "Don't say anything."

The car came to a stop just in front of me. "Christian, such a surprise to see you here. We're about to serve the notice to vacate." Janet climbed from the car and the tension inside Christian must have seized me.

"It's my home. You can't just evict me." I lunged, but Christian held me firm.

"Oh, I can. I am. You've got thirty days to vacate." She shoved an envelope into my hand. I wanted to drop it on the ground and Janet grinned, clearly aware of the turmoil within me.

"Get out of here." I hurled the words at the woman as I pulled away from Christian, but his grip, biting and sharp, was firm.

"Don't play her game, Tabs."

Grief and fury tore at me, shredding me from within. "She can't do this!"

"I can and I am." The grin Janet shot me was saccharine, all fake and uncaring, and that stoked the fires inside my belly.

"Get lost, Janet!" Christian wrenched me toward the door of his car, but I didn't want to budge. Every step was against my will, while Janet, the bitch, laughed.

"Oh, I'm going. But don't think you can beat us on this one, because we've waited a long time for this opportunity." A flash of lightning, the curious purple-red, split the sky. Janet looked up, bared her teeth and gave a laugh, then she spun on her out-of-place heels and trotted back to the car, hips swinging and hair bobbing up and down. Every carefully placed step fanned the red-hot fires scouring me from the inside out.

It was only as the car reversed back up the lane that I allowed myself to sag, the metal of the car holding me up. The righteous indignation that burned me fizzled away, leaving me limp. "Why? How?"

"I don't know Tabs, but I think we need to get out of here and find out what we have." He reached up, cupped one cheek, and I gazed into his eyes. "We'll get through this. We'll help the Captain and Alice."

He opened the car door, eased me in and shut it gently, before circling the car and climbing in himself. "Let's go home."

Three words that had never before sounded so good.

# CHAPTER 16

Christian and I had lugged the packet and trunk into the house. At the end of our efforts, I felt grimy, exhausted and completely disheartened. Seeing Janet, being evicted, sliced a hole in my mind and heart.

Unable to plan, to think or even find something to look forward to was new to me.

I headed for the bathroom, shut the door and stripped off my dirt-streaked clothes. Every action was slow, laborious, and I needed to work hard to focus on every step. Turning on the taps, I sighed and waited for the billowing steam to begin.

I stepped in and my muscles relaxed as the warm water sluiced down my body. The fog continued to obstruct my thinking, so when a sound caught my attention, I turned, almost losing my footing as Christian tugged me towards him.

He steadied me and I gripped both his shoulders, as my body registered his nakedness firmly against mine. "Careful."

"Christian? I'm just..."

"Shhh." He kissed me. The touch gentle while his lips brushed mine.

Even before I could extrapolate that my body was reacting to him, he spun me toward the wall. "Close your eyes."

I did and soon I felt his hands, massaging a thick substance—shampoo, offered my beleaguered brain—into my hair. The scent of apples wafted. He worked up a lather, paying careful attention to my skull. The egg there had settled, but I shied as he rinsed my hair. No man had ever done this for me, and I found the action to be both endearing and arousing.

The web he wound around me replaced the odd disconnection I'd felt since arriving home. That thought caught my breath and attention. I attempted to consider it, but the touch of his hands moving to my shoulders awoke the hunger that never seemed to fully abated around him.

"Christian—"

"Shhh." Again, he stopped my words, his small caress, the whisper of his breath on my back left me shivering in anticipation. His hands slid over my body, unceasing yet gentle. My knees wobbled as sensations flooded me. I started when he reached beyond me and turned off the taps. For a moment I was lost.

"Christian?"

I could feel the jut of his erection against my bottom, hard and probing, but he carefully propelled me from the stall. *Have I done something wrong?* I bit my lip and glanced at him. His smile broke through the diamond hardness of his lips as if he held his emotions in a firm but slipping grip. "What?"

"You needed a shower and I promised myself I'd care for you."

I didn't want that, so I reached out, but he shuffled away—my fingers barely glanced over his flesh. "Nah ah ah." This time his grin was more carefree.

"Go on. Get dressed while I clean up, then I'll make dinner and we can start looking at the contents of today's find."

With that he enveloped me in a towel, shunted me out of the bedroom to the hall and closed the door with a thud, all before I could argue that I wanted him.

Even as I opened my mouth, as I stared at the wooden panel real life intruded. I closed my mouth, gave a small shrug, and grinned while I listened for the sound of the shower being re-engaged. Only then did I move to the bedroom.

# CHAPTER 17

We worked together, Christian and I, preparing a quick and satisfying dinner. Salad with grilled fish from his freezer, but it wasn't the main concern this evening. The chest we'd discovered haunted us. Jeered in silence and demanded our full attention. With that in mind, we ate without discussion, both of us needing to know exactly what we'd discovered.

Once we'd cleared away and washed up, we hunkered down and he reached for the simple latch. No lock existed, and it was clear he never expected the property to be breached or resumed. "It's amazing he must have placed such importance on the promise of the Colonial Office. He never locked the chest."

I blew slightly, and a waft of dust and cobwebs flew wide.

Christian coughed, and I grimaced. "Sorry about that."

"I'll be okay in a moment." He coughed again and reached for the glass of water on the small coffee table beside him. He drank deep and the movement of his Adams apple drew my eye. My mouth dried as I gazed on his beauty. *Would I ever get to the point where I didn't appreciate the look of him?* The way he treated me like I was the most important woman in his life. It was also how I felt about him.

He turned and must have caught me watching him, and his grin grew wide. "Like what you see?"

Loss of words was new to me but the feelings that fluttered through me, the depth of them—or was it because I was finally ready to acknowledge what seemed to have grown inside me for a while—shattered my usual air of self-possession.

"I... Uh... Maybe when we're done here, we could talk?" The words ended on a scratchy high note, totally betraying my discomfort, and Christian's grin died away.

"Are you okay?" He scooted closer and held out a hand.

I gave a chuckle of discomfort. "Yeah, but I'd like to sort this first." I looked meaningfully to the chest and he pierced me with one last deep look, then turned away, looking back to the casket and flipped the old metal tab. With both hands, he levered the lid. It squeaked and groaned in response. For a moment we both just stared. There was clothing, a book and there in the middle a small jewel case.

I reached out, needing to touch it.

"Wait. Let's lay everything on the floor before we open it." Christian spoke evenly, and in that instant reality slammed into me. The Captain had showed us some of his memories. Although this wasn't the packet we'd seen, it could be anything and a little wariness wouldn't go astray.

"You're right, Christian. I've just got used to forging ahead."

He turned to me and winked. "That's okay, Tabs. But its better if we take our time and work through this in an organized fashion." From his pocket he withdrew a camera and snapped some shots. "We can show them to the professor when he gets here."

Bit by bit, Christian removed every item and laid them on the floor. The clothing was a mix of women's and men's. "Do you think he was bringing this back for her?"

Christian shook his head. "Remember, we don't know where he was lost, so I'd say it's safe to say that she packed it away and stashed it under the house."

I bit my lip and considered his words. "But then, how did the package get here? I mean, as far as we know, the Captain was lost before he delivered the item to Alice. Maybe we need to go back and check her journals."

Yet, even as I spoke, I felt there was something missing that would put all the blocks in place. I reached for my notepad and flicked through, but without anything concrete to go on, I rose and moved to the table where I'd left my laptop and retreated back to my chair. It only took a moment to boot up the computer and find the correct file.

I scanned the files, particularly the notations beside the journal entries, but as time moved on, my vision grew cloudy. When I felt the touch of a hand on my shoulder, I looked up.

Looming above me was Christian, and he held the computer in his hand. The one I'd been using. I gazed blearily at him. "What?"

"You were asleep, and the computer nearly fell. Let's get some rest. It's not going away."

"But I should—"

"We're tired, Tabs. Let's rest and tackle this again in the morning." Christian was right, of course. We'd be fresh after sleeping and we'd most likely find the information we sought then.

So, I rose, took the hand he stretched out to me and together we headed for the bedroom.

*B*efore me stood Alice, her gown of gray edged in a severe black cord. Her hair streaked with gray and her face pulled tight.

*"You came and found me. Thank you, Tabitha. Your efforts will not be in vain."*

*I shook my head, lost for a moment and cast my gaze around, yet the surroundings were hazy and gray and I know this was yet another dream. Another time where I was visited by those who'd passed many years before my birth.*

*"You've found the package, but you have to understand great danger lies ahead now. Please, you'll need help to take the next step."* Alice's voice reached out to me and tugged deeply at my psyche. *"He sent it to me before the end. His trunk was delivered, full of silk and items. Things he'd bought for me."*

*Now her face turned ravaged with grief and its twin emotion lodged deeply inside my chest, squeezing as if I too felt her pain and loss. "I didn't want them. I'd much rather he'd brought them himself, but the man who delivered them... He told me that the Captain had disappeared from his lodgings and he'd been charged with the safe delivery of the items it contained. I know it isn't true, but I'm so far away and so much time has elapsed already."*

*"But Alice—"*

*She gave a shake of her head, cutting off my words. "With that I had to be grateful. Yet, my captain had written one last letter, and it told me that sometime, in the future someone would come. Someone who would know how to safely see the package to its destination when the time came." Her face, bone white, shone in the half light, the silvery tracks of her tears declaring just how much this cost her.*

*My heart stuttered. "But I don't know—"*

*Then, as if he'd just realized—or found a way inside this realm—Christian appeared in the dream beside me. "I will make sure it's done, Alice. I have contacts who know the appropriate steps to take. His efforts will not be in vain."*

*In my dream, I felt Christian reach around my shoulders, the sense of his comforting the nerves that threatened to overcome me. But it also soothed the raggedness that tore at me.*

*I reached out, touched her hand in this dream world, hoping to convey a little a surety that we would finally see this done. "We will do everything we can, Alice. Please, believe that."*

*She smiled, a tremulous curve of her lips. "They will come, my friends. The evil ones. They did before, looking for the package. They will do anything, take any step. But they cloak themselves in danger, hate and sly ways. They won't show who or what they really are, instead they will be furtive and hide. They will promise to assist. Do not believe them and above all do not relinquish that package. He paid with his life. You may too, and this time, there may be no way out. For any of us." Alice gave a final nod, wavering as if holding the form exhausted her, then she winked out.*

*A snuffed candle.*

# CHAPTER 18

*I* woke, gasping and breathless.

"Christian?" I reached, my hands touching flesh. Warm and reassuring.

"Tab–?"

I wanted to burrow into his arms and find safety. I took a moment and breathed deeply. We hadn't declared any kind of undying love, so it was better to restrain myself and deal internally, I told myself. But it took a moment to drag the strength around me like a cloak. "It wasn't a dream. I know it. She talks to me, they both do. But that package." I shook my head, certain now that only we could change what happened. "It's more than we could ever imagine."

Christian scrubbed his hands over his face, as if looking for a way to come to terms with what he'd seen and experienced. "Let's go get some breakfast and a coffee. I think better after the first drink of the day."

I knew he was trying to install some form of levity into the situation, but I couldn't manage that. Not yet. The horror I'd felt chilled me all the way to the center of my bones.

*Dwelling on it won't make it better.* "Perhaps you're right. Something to eat and drink might let me re-evaluate this." Not that I expected it to.

Instead I rolled, slid to the side of the bed and jumped to my feet. "Ow!"

He was around, quick as a flash. "What happened?"

I grimaced. "I jarred my ankle, is all." The heat of embarrassment flared on my skin and he slid a gentle finger over my cheek.

"Be careful. I like you whole and healthy." His gaze dove deep into my eyes and for a moment I fancied there was more, a deeper commitment. Then I gave a silent snort, because it was wishful thinking on my part.

He helped me up, and I hobbled to the kitchen with him then settled into a seat as he moved around, totally comfortable making breakfast for us.

Within minutes a rack of toast, butter and spreads was joined by two deep cups of fragrant coffee. I inhaled deeply and picked up my mug. "So, where do we start?"

"You were going to tell me your impressions of the dream, then I was going to offer mine."

"Okay. I think Alice is terrified the *whatever it is*, will fall into the wrong hands. It's clearly of great religious significance and power, the way they seem to be after it. Or have been." I bit my lip, because this all sounded so totally far-fetched and unbelievable.

Christian plonked down in the seat on the opposite side of the table and it shuddered. "I think you're correct." He drank some coffee and sighed. "You're right, it does sound fantastical, yet we've now met with ghosts and when combined with what's going on with your home, after all these years I'm sure that we're dealing with something of great mystical importance. Add to that what I did glean from the professor, all we can be sure of is that we don't know a lot about what it is. This whole situation smells like day old fish left in the sun."

He sounded as bewildered by the mess as I was. I couldn't help myself, I reached out, placed my hand over his and squeezed. As much as I needed reassurance, I thought he probably did too because we were walking a fine line here. Either we were totally stupid or totally gullible, and neither of those positions were palatable. Even in the depths of my frustration I knew the danger loomed real and close and it made me consider what could potentially go wrong. "The one thing I do think, it that Kira shouldn't be here right now." I bit my lip, waiting for him to reprimand me, and tell me it wasn't my place, yet Christian gave a small jerky nod.

"Yes, I agree. I'll ring Peta and ask if she can keep her for a few more days. Whatever happens, I don't want her hurt and the best way to manage that is to send her away."

I took a bite of the toast I'd buttered, but it was tasteless and dry, like eating sawdust. "I'm really not hungry."

"Neither am I, but given this mess, we need to keep some kind of normality to our lives. And we're going to need strength to get through what comes next. Eat up and we can go through the rest of the trunk's contents."

Slowly, with deliberation, I bit, chewed and swallowed my way through the food, even though my stomach roiled. I drank down my drink, letting it moisten the hard-dry food I'd eaten.

By the end of the meal, though, I felt a little better and offered to wash up, freeing Christian to make the phone call about Kira.

We settled in the lounge, me in the chair with my laptop and Christian hunched over the trunk. "You list what we find in the order and photograph. I'll lay everything out and check to see if anything is hidden."

I chewed my lip, unsure how I felt now that the moment was here.

The trunk lid was cracked open, and I peered in, while Christian wielded tiny digital camera.

*Click.*

The first photo taken, I peered within and noted the careful, almost loving way the trunk was packed. Everything folded and in tiny calico bags. They contained sprigs of what looked like rosemary and lavender. Another leaf, she supposed was mint rounded out the mix.

"Why would they have herbs in here?"

Christian grinned widely. "Rosemary and lavender keep away cockroaches and moths. The mint is, I think, for mice."

"Hmm. And you know that, how?" She couldn't restrain the mirth in her words.

"Goes with the territory, Tabs. I'm trained as a researcher. Marine or other, I have to have a decent knowledge of storage techniques and the history of storage and packing, so I know what I'm doing and handling."

I harrumphed and placed the tiny fragile bag on the plastic sheet he'd rolled out and turned my attention back to the job at hand.

Dresses and undergarments, a journal which Christian carefully opened then placed to the side with a casual, 'household information' joined the sachets pile which now towered. Toward the bottom we found a small satchel, wrapped in stained cloth.

"Oil cloth," Christian told me when I loomed over his shoulder.

I reached out, but a buzz met my fingers and I pulled back. "What on earth?"

I reached again, but Christian caught my hand. "No. Leave it be. I think it's the item we needed to find, but it is like it's warning us not to touch it."

My stomach bottomed out at the thought.

"So, what do we do next?"

"We wait."

I shifted in my chair, uncomfortable with the 'wait and see' method. I needed to know, but he was right, I conceded. We needed someone who knew what they were doing. "When is the Professor due?"

"He just said soon."

I was about to argue that wasn't exactly definitive when he grunted, "Did you finish going through Alice's journal?"

Christian's words tugged me from my introspection.

"Uh, almost. I only have a few pages left. Why?"

"Perhaps there's something in them, Tabs. I have the feeling that there is more we need to learn. Besides, the professor will want as much information as we can give him."

I stood up quickly, and a tiny spear of vertigo affected me. "Tabs?"

"I'm okay. Just stood up too quickly. Let's just find the journal then, and sort that out." He didn't move though, only stared at me as if reading what had caused that flash.

"You're sure you're okay?"

I grinned, feeling improved already. "Quite."

We wandered to the bedroom, hand in hand, and I only let go when we entered the room. I'd dropped the journal on the bedside table and sat down, felt the dip as he lowered himself beside me.

My mouth dried. Sudden hunger rose, clawing deep inside my belly as the waft of his personal cologne filled the air.

Heady and musky, and all Christian.

I licked my lips and turned at his groan. "Tabs..."

His lips descended, soft and hard at the same time. Demanding. Wanting. Hungry.

Now I burrowed in, taking and giving, lip-to-lip so that we somehow ended up flat on the bed. "Christian, I want you." I couldn't stop the words—the emotions were honest and hungry. Heaven knew, the desire which licked at me since I'd met him, demanded more from both of us. The ache and emptiness between my legs and the hollowness in my gut spurred me on.

I reached up, tugged at his shirt, but his fingers shoved mine aside. With a quick jerk, the cotton was up and over his head, discarded as I fumbled with the buttons on my shirt.

The last gave as he covered my hands with his, gently pulling them away. "Let me." The tremble of his voice rippled over me, spurring me on. The tips of his fingers slid over the mounds of my breast, separated from my flesh by the simple white material of my bra, but still I arched, demanding more.

I slid my hands beneath my back, searching for the clasp as he drew me closer, chest to chest. "Let me."

The caress of his breath over my neck had senses splintering, and I groaned. "Please."

The clasp gave. My breasts released from their confinement and the lycra sagged. He burrowed under the cups, fingertips search for and finding my nipples, where they gently grazed the sensitized flesh.

My legs trembled as did the rest of my body, which heated to almost incendiary heights as he groped at the fastener of my shorts. Once undone he slid soft hands inside my underwear, tugging until I was naked and displayed for him.

"Tabitha, you're so beautiful." His voice shook as I closed my eyes. Behind my lids I could see him still, the vision in my imagination only a pale shadow of how gorgeous he really was. Miles of golden flesh, well-developed muscles and his piercing blue eyes.

I opened my mouth, and he was there. His tongue surging between my lips, demanding everything I had to give. Dampness tickled my thighs, telling me how ready I was for him, for this intimate act between two lovers. The feel of his hand, searching and questing before carefully invading the part of my body I shared only with him, hurled me further into the maelstrom. "Please." My words were a plea, an entreaty.

The emptiness grew. Only Christian could fill it and me. Make me whole.

My hand moved, cupping the back of his head, holding him close so I could feast on the taste of him. Coffee, a hint of raspberry conserve and man. My nipples grazed his chest and ripples of sensation, like tiny bolts of lightning arced through me.

I urged him on, sliding a hand down his abdomen until I found his jutting cock. A touch, little more than a glance against his flesh, had him rearing back, hissing. The tiny droplet of fluid on the head of his cock told me just how ready he was.

He moved, jerking and tugging the rest of his clothing free from where it had pooled, and he released me. I opened my eyes in time to see him lean up and over. "I need you now, Tabs."

My legs widened to accommodate him, and he fitted himself, then slid deep inside my body.

I screamed as a million tiny nerves and muscles contracted and released, the orgasm stronger than any I'd ever experienced while Christian moved, frenzied.

Starving.

I held tight, watching the cording of his neck, the way his eyes closed, letting sensation after sensation wash over me.

He didn't stop though, his hands firmed and slid, feeding the fever once more until I too spun away, lost in the hectic moment.

The fire inside me grew, boiled and demanded as we rocked together. I grabbed his shoulders, held on tight until both of us stilled, bodies heaving and wet.

The explosion between us stilled everything.

The world stopped. There was only Christian and I.

One breath.

Another.

Each sucked oxygen into our exhausted bodies, still tightly entwined as we wanted.

It had been cataclysmic. Earthy and yet more than that.

For a moment, I was sure I'd shared a piece of my soul with this man who held me tight. What's more, I couldn't and wouldn't regret it.

"Tabs, I..."

I wasn't ready to hear him tell me this wasn't right. That we shouldn't continue down this path, so I laid a finger against his lips, stopping the words before they formed. Because right wrong or even indifferent, I loved Christian.

In that moment, the truth was undeniable.

# CHAPTER 19

$\mathcal{C}$hristian slept and I stared at the ceiling.

Anxiety swam through me. I'd just lived through the most spectacular loving in history. Evil dogged us as we strove to work out what we'd received and how to stop some kind of ultimate evil from gaining possession of it. I was in love with a man who enjoyed the sexual intimacy without the emotional connection. Or a condom, it seemed.

He thought he loved me.

I knew I loved him.

*How the hell do I sort this mess out?* Of course, there was no answer, so I closed my eyes, breathed deep and considered that if these things were approached in a rational and sequential order, then one of these conundrums might be solved.

I reached for Alice's diary. "Plenty of time to deal with the rest once we get to the bottom of this."

I'd felt threatened in the past, but now, there was a cloying sense of danger. It was stronger than when Janet had turned up. It was as if it was hoping to slide into the house, through the doors and windows. Pressure built in my ears, but I simply gripped the book, flipping to the final pages, and settled in to read.

*The Captain's friend, Mr. Arthur Harmson, brought me a small package today. He brought me Michael's trunk too, filled with the most beautiful items. Things he'd purchased for me and nestled within was also his final request. To care for the package until my dying days and to pass it on to be cared for. Mr. Harmson schooled me greatly as to its care and importance. That it is of great significance but must never be revealed.*

*My Michael seems to have undertaken much more difficult and dangerous work than he'd ever given me to understand. That last time, he'd clearly been worried, and on the occasions where I'd spied his concern, he'd been grave, and yet he brushed those fears aside for my benefit. Only now, when it's too late, do I understand.*

*I will not commit to this journal the location of the item, only that I've followed the directions to the letter.*

*Michael loved me. Made provision for my safety even though his danger was extreme. Surely such a man will find his reward in the bosom of our Lord. His body may be lost, but I remain assured that his legacy will live on.*

*I rejoice in knowing that he's at rest, but fear that my soul now will be prey to sorrow and regrets.*

*That our child stirs in his bed, never having known his father, or his knowledge of our child fills me with grief.*

*What do I tell our son? How do I ensure that he has the opportunity to know his father for the good and great man he was?*

*I am forbidden to reveal anything to him of his father's mission until such time as he can be taught the safeguards Mr. Harmson has suggested. The training and how to prepare the house so it remains a haven. In that I must agree. For the safety of everyone. Time passes slowly and I fear I will never again know the happiness that once suffused my soul.*

*A*

*I* bit my lip, understanding that Alice had felt desolation, loneliness and grief without her family or any support. I knew what I'd suffered at the loss of my father, and the deep well of despair that had followed was so much less than her sense of loss. My gaze automatically swung in the direction of Christian and cold seeped into my bones. Considering his loss was immeasurable and dark.

Cloying in intensity.

A sob lodged in my throat, threatening to escape, but I muffled it as I bit down on my hand.

I didn't want Christian to wake and find me like that. It would lead to far too many questions of the sort I wasn't prepared to answer right now.

With great care, I rose. My clothes were scattered all over the floor and I carefully picked them up, the journal still clutched against my chest, and I snuck out of the room.

Once in the bathroom, I turned on the shower and let the torrent flow even as I placed the journal on the vanity unit.

Pain, mine or hers I couldn't say, burst from me along with the sobs that wracked my body as I fumbled for and locked the door. Finally spent, I reached up and turned off the faucet before I slid to the floor, my chest still heaving but the violence passed. A knock at the door grabbed my attention. "Tabs? Let me in?"

I shook my head, hair whipping back and forth until I realized he couldn't hear that. "No. I'm uh... I'm showering."

It was a feeble attempt at best, and he knocked again. Clearly, he didn't intend to leave me be. "Tabs, please. Tell me what's wrong."

I scrubbed my hands over my throbbing eyes. "I don't want to." I hung my head.

"Tabitha, let me in or I'll break the door down." Christian sounded so totally calm, yet I couldn't miss the steely intention in his voice.

"Just... Just give me a minute." I hauled myself up, hating the weakness that led to me giving in and unlocking the door. Even as the click sounded the doorknob turned and he pushed his way in.

"Dammit Tabs, what's wrong? What happened?"

"I read her journal, Christian. The last page tore me up, and you were asleep." Now my excuse sounded lame, and I hung my head, feeling a measure of shame at the weakness.

"You should have woken me." He slid a gentle finger under my chin and raised it so I couldn't avoid his gaze.

"I'm sorry."

"Dammit." He tugged me against him, our bodies touching intimately as he enfolded me in his arms. "I want to be there for you, Tabitha, and you need to give me that choice."

A tiny sob erupted from my chest.

"I told you at the beginning, I wanted you. That comes with all the emotional baggage you could ever imagine. Don't ever hide what hurts you from me again." He kissed the top of my head as I slumped against him. "Don't lock me out, Tabs. Please."

## CHAPTER 20

*L*unch was cooking, and I inhaled the wafting smell of sausages on the grill while making the salad. Christian and I hadn't talked fully about what had happened in the bedroom and bathroom. I felt raw, as if my emotions had scratched their way to the surface.

Instead, by unspoken agreement, we'd tabled that discussion for later. When other distractions were dealt with.

As I pulled the plates from the cupboard, the sound of the doorbell chimed. I glanced at Christian, wondering if it was Janet—my stomach wobbled at that thought— or someone else he expected.

"That's probably the Professor. Could you get it for me?" I gulped at Christian's request but nodded and hurried up the short hallway, my feet slapping on the tiled floor, the tiny limp from my healing ankle barely noticeable unless I rushed.

I cracked the door open and, on the step, stood an older man, in his sixth decade or so. "Can I help you?"

"Yes, my name is Professor Leggett and Christian asked me to come."

He was so earnest that without thought I opened the door wide. "Please come in."

I closed and latched the door after him and showed him through to the kitchen. "Well, Christian, here I am at your request." He stopped still and sputtered. "Oh dear, I seem to have come at a most inconvenient time."

"Not at all, Professor Leggett. Welcome. Why don't you join us for lunch, and we can discuss what we know before I show you what we have?"

The man—slightly stooped, with bushy white eyebrows and thinning hair—glanced in my direction. I couldn't stop myself from smiling. He was perhaps not quite as trim as a department store actor, but with the same grandfatherly softness that reminded me of Santa. An aura of calmness that emanated from him. "Please join us. I can grab another plate from the cupboard. What would you like to drink?"

"You must be the young lady Christian was telling me about. The one who contacted him?"

I nodded. "Yes. I inherited the house from my father and started to..." Now I stopped, unsure what or where to even begin. He needed the facts and I was struggling so wordlessly beseeched Christian.

"Sorry, professor. This is Tabitha, and she inherited the cottage from her father. There was an agreement set in place with the Colonial Office that up until now has been honored."

The professor quirked an eyebrow. "Was?"

"Long story." Christian placed the platter of sausages down beside the salads and dressings before sliding his hand over mine and gave a half nod. "Anyway, as I told you, her dreams and mine are now coming faster than ever. We've retrieved Alice's journal, found letters, and are slowly putting the facts together based on the information we've been receiving through the dreams. We know the item is important and time is of the essence as the attempts to take control of the property have stepped up as well. Who or whatever they are, obviously want it and haven't yet worked out that we've retrieved the package, but that won't last long. I believe we need to act with urgency."

"Hmm. And you've got all the documentation? The letters and journals?" The professor rubbed his brow as if thinking hard over the information we'd shared.

"Since then Professor, we've found more. And of course, the item itself." Christian speared a sausage, cut off a small piece, and chewed.

"Is the artefact safe? Have you opened it?" The professor leaned forward, concern tugging his brows together as he stared at us.

I shook my head, strands of hair whipping me in the face. "No. The information was specific. It shouldn't be opened by anyone other than the person it was intended for. Christian put it in a safe location, so even if someone did get in, they wouldn't know where to begin their search."

Christian smiled, filling me with a warm glow.

"Then you've clearly done the right thing. Let's finish this excellent repast then we can investigate what you've found."

Food now tasted once more like sawdust. The act of eating however allowed me to concentrate and distract myself from the other, far more serious considerations.

Once we'd finished, I rose, collected the bowls and plates, filled the dishwasher then joined the men in the lounge room, where we'd left things in careful piles.

"This is the journal of Alice. It tells us a little about the story of how they met, and the house. Tabs has made a quick ready reference if you'd like to take a look." Christian held out the sheaf of papers I'd carefully printed from my notes.

The professor settled into the chair and scanned the notes. "Interesting," and "hmm," were the choice of comment. We waited until he looked up.

"Yes, well, that gives us some information. Letters?"

Christian handed them to the professor who once more examined what we'd given him.

The knock started on the door. Insistent. I looked at Christian and he frowned. "I'll go." Then he rose while I watched, a feeling of presentiment flashing through me. The timing of this intrusion both odd and disquieting.

"No, Janet. I'm sorry, but I'm busy." His voice forceful as if filtered from the front door.

"Christian, I'm coming in." Janet. *Bitch*.

I glanced at the Professor. He rose, reaching into his pocket for something. A vial I noted with surprise, and he moved swiftly in Christian's direction. I stayed where I was, instinct telling me to protect the items before me.

Voices rose, demanding, then afraid.

My stomach wobbled, and I glanced toward the entryway. I couldn't see anything but heard Christian. "Janet?" The shock reverberated through me. Whatever he'd seen surprised him. Left him reeling.

It took only seconds for these revelations to come to me and I rose, meaning to go to him.

*Tabitha, you must stay where you are. Protect these artefacts. Too much is at stake. It's gone too far now.*

The Captain's words sounded as if he were beside me, yet no sound filled the air. He was communicating directly to my mind and I don't know how he did it. There was no misunderstanding the urgency in his words either. So, I stayed still, as if my feet were set in concrete.

The door slammed and I winced at the ferocity of the sound. "She'll be back, Christian," the professor warned him.

I craned, listening hard so I could work out what happened. What I hadn't heard or seen.

"But what was it? That wasn't Janet..." Bewilderment echoed in Christian's words.

"It was, my boy. That's the real Janet. You were married to her for how long?"

They rounded the corner together and I moved, my legs finally unsticking from where I'd waited through the altercation.

"A couple of years." Christian's eyes had glazed over and he shook his head. "What is she? Or it? I mean, how could I not know?" His voice arced up on the last word, disbelief written on his face with wide-open eyes, and he shook his head.

"She's a demon, my boy. Not a full one judging by the damage I did her—and for that we should be grateful. But that's what makes her so dangerous. They control what you see and hear. That's how she fooled you for so many years, but we need to work quickly now." The professor set about pulling things from his leather satchel.

"How do you..." Christian stopped, his entire body rigid as a thought must have occurred to him. "You're guessing?" Disbelief colored his tones. Grasping Christian's hand, I felt the shake and shudder of his body.

The Professor sighed heavily. "I can feel it. The evil that surrounds us right now. I've been doing this for a long time and know what to look for. How they—these demons— react. Besides, I employed an old trick. I dampened my hands with consecrated water before touching her shoulder. You saw the way she jerked back, Christian. It burned only one of us, which is how I knew definitively of her demon origins. But yes, I did guess at the beginning."

"What happened?" My gaze settled on the Professor.

"It seems Christian here was married to a demon."

I blinked in disbelief. "But that would make Kira..." Biting my lip, I considered the information the professor shared. Janet was a demon, or at least part one. That meant—

"What about Kira?" Christian's voice dripped with ice. Equal parts fury and terror if I didn't miss my guess.

"Who?" The professor leaned close.

"My daughter." Christian spoke hoarsely, and I frowned, not having meant to make the situation worse.

My gut clenched. Kira was a kid. A great kid and there was no way... I shook my head. "No." There was no way.

The Professor cleared his throat. "It's more than likely, Christian. Just think about what I'm saying."

A flash of inspiration hit. "Is there some way we can assist or prepare?" Changing the subject and bringing them both back to the job at hand would certainly help in clearing the air for now.

"We call in a priest. A specialist. I know one. Give me a minute." The professor whipped out his mobile phone and scrolled, then pressed a button, holding up his hand to tell them it was ringing.

"Fergus! How are you?" The professor hunched away and gave a laugh. "Yeah, I know. That was fun, wasn't it? But I've got a bit of a problem. I have an artefact that is in a private citizen's possession. We've just had a half demon attempt entry. This demon groomed one of the citizens for years, going so far as to marry and give birth to offspring."

He listened carefully, nodding and 'hmming' before speaking again. "It's powerful and I have an inkling of what it is, but I won't speak its name until I'm sure we have it adequately protected." Another pause where the professor frowned, making a deep v with his brows.

A crash sounded at the door, followed by a roar of anger. The windows rattled and the ceiling shuddered. The professor whipped around and stared at Christian.

The professor looked up, startled, before a look of satisfaction settled. "Just a minute, Fergus." The professor cupped his phone and stared at Christian. "You had the house blessed?"

Christian shook his head. "No. Not me."

"That explains it then. She could enter because she's not fully of demon blood. He can't." Swiping his hand from the speaker, he lifted the phone back to his ear. "Fergus, this is important. We've just had an attempted incursion into the house. How soon can you get here?"

Whatever the answer was, the Professor gave a tiny scowl then hung up. "Tomorrow morning. We need to make it through tonight. Where is your child?"

"At my sister's."

"Here on the island?" The professor rubbed his hand over his eyes.

"Yeah."

"Either get her to the mainland and I'll give you an address or to the church. You do have one, right?"

Christian stood rigid with fury. "Why?"

"Because she's at risk. If Janet goes after her and whatever just tried to get in here does, then she's going to be the next best thing."

The blood drained from Christian's face. "What about if I bring her here?"

"Into this mess? No. She's better off away. A priest will know what to do. Get me a number for the church, and we'll find a way to deal with this mess."

Christian disappeared, only coming back with a page in his shaking hand. "Here. It's the latest newsletter. Number's at the top."

Needing to do something, I ushered him to the chair. "Ring Peta. Have her take Kira to the church. I'll grab you a drink while you do that."

But his hands shook. "I..." His face changed from a pale white to a sickly green. "Ring." He thrust the phone at me as he rushed from the room.

I couldn't quite understand how he felt, but I felt keenly the need to get Kira to a safe location. I found the contacts and dialed.

"Hey, what's up Christian?" Peta answered, her voice bright.

"It's Tabs. We have a situation, and I need you to do something without asking a ton of questions. You need to get Kira to the church. Someone there will be waiting for her."

The line turned silent for a moment. Then Peta laughed. "Oh, it's not Halloween yet, Tabs."

I swiped a hand over my face. If this, the chest pounding terror that was inching through me was anything to go by, then no wonder Christian was throwing up. I looked up as he returned to the room. He took the phone.

"It's no joke, Peta. For her sake and yours, get her to the church. Now." He infused his terror into the words, and I hoped she'd do so. He waited, listening to whatever she was saying, then nodded and hung up. "She's going now."

We waited long moments. Tension so thick it coated me and everything around us in an almost viscous layer.

Professor Leggett settled on the lounge chair. "We should have a break. Do you think your sister is at the Church yet?"

I glanced at Christian; his face screwed up tight. "I hope so. I'll give her another couple of minutes, then check."

We waited, moments ticking by, accompanied by the clock.

He dialed, engaged the speaker function. "Peta?"

"We're... We're here but Christian. Something *happened*." Her voice sounded like a hiss down the phone and hairs stood on end.

"Is Kira safe?" He demanded, and in my mind, I could see Peta nodding.

"Yes. But outside there're things in the shadows. They tried to grab us. Kira... She waved her hand, her eyes glowed! What's going on Christian?"

"I can't answer. Not now. Tomorrow... You have to stay there until tomorrow. Help is on the way. Just stay inside and keep Kira with you. You're okay as long as you do that, right Professor?"

The older man nodded. "Yes, but it's vitally important. If the priest is there, have him spray holy water on all doors and windows. Have him bless Kira too."

"Sure. Yes. Okay. But Christian, are we safe? Like really safe."

The professor took the phone from Christian's hands. "Miss Monteith, Peta, yes?"

"Who is this?"

"Professor Leggett. A friend of your brothers. You will be safe as long as you both remain inside. No matter what you see, hear or even smell, remain within the building, but of the utmost importance is the child. Do not let them take her."

I quivered with concern, sharing it with the man who looked poleaxed. I knew Christian wanted to protect his daughter and hated asking Peta to assume the responsibility. I saw the guilt riding his brow.

When we hung up the phone I settled in beside Christian. Not quite touching because I wasn't sure right now if he'd accept my touch, but near enough in case he needed me.

The hours passed in relative silence, and from time to time the heavy pull of sleep would have me nodding off. Each time I woke, it was to a thud or the sound of Janet's screaming for Christian to let her in. With each hour that passed, his face grew progressively grimmer.

I'd fallen asleep again and woke as Christian called my name softly. Blinking, I looked around, unrefreshed.

Light shone through the windows as dawn broke and the Professor stood. "We should check outside now."

Christian and I rose. "But—" he started to object, but the Professor waved his hands.

"Daylight will weaken her. But if they can cover the sun..." He shrugged. "Time is of the essence now that we know what they are."

"Cover the sun?"

"Eclipse or even heavy cloud cover. We need to hurry. Get over to the church." The Professor prodded us forward.

# CHAPTER 21

Fergus was indeed a special priest. Grizzled and old, with shrewd blue eyes hidden behind heavy glasses, I guessed him to be somewhere around late sixties, though still very spry. He rolled up in a heavy old Mercedes that appeared to be at least thirty years old. It was, however, immaculate inside and out, and featured a large trunk full of hard old-fashioned cases.

"Fergus!" The professor welcomed him with a hug and the priest grinned.

"So, you finally got me to one of the islands. Seems someone arranged for the ferry to wait a little longer than usual, so I'd make it? And you'd better introduce me to these nice young people waiting."

Once the niceties were attended to, we moved inside, packing up the last of the items the professor deemed necessary.

We would have traveled in one car, but the priest was adamant that his vehicle had everything he required, and it wouldn't fit into the car Christian drove. Nor would we fit in it.

We led the way, and I sat in the front, balancing a picnic basket. I'd argued Peta and Kira would likely be famished. It made sense as they'd rushed out into the night unprepared. I just hoped they'd been warm enough.

We came around the corner and stopped. A large log blocking our way. I made to open the door, but the professor stopped me. "Just wait a minute," he instructed, and Fergus climbed from his car, already donned with robes, chains and heaven knew what else.

The man inched forward and I don't know why, but I squeaked, because I half expected something to jump out of the scraggly bushes that surrounded the trunk.

As I watched, they shook and shivered. I noted Fergus had a book open in his hand, the other raised, and the hair on the nape of my neck stood on end.

The sky changed color even as we watched, turning a mauvy-black. "We should help him," I breathed.

The professor shook his head. "Not yet. He'll let us know when." He spoke so calmly and yet, the panic in the bottom of my stomach really didn't abate, just churned slowly. I bit my lip and Christian gripped my hand hard.

The man moved back and forth, his hands dipping and moving in a slow cadence. It was mesmeric, or would have been if not for the terror congealing in my belly.

Moments passed, then with a final nod, Fergus turned and made his way to the car.

Christian wound down the window. "Do we need to move the log now?"

The priest hurried forward, shaking his head emphatically. "No. We need to find a way around this blockage. I've bound what's here, but it won't hold them forever and we should hurry to the church."

Christian rubbed his hands over his bleared eyes. "There's no other way, unless we travel on foot."

The priest stared at him, as if what Christian suggested was somehow unbelievable. "No. I need all my cases, so I can be prepared. Isn't there another way?"

The underbrush was low, and I saw the way Christian was eyeing it off. "We go through the bush, then."

I wondered if either the priest or the professor realized the import of what he'd just suggested. Christian was a protector. Of the reef, the environment, and particularly this island. To suggest he'd drive through the scrub... it betrayed just how disturbed he was by the situation.

Fergus hurried back to his vehicle, and Christian backed up a little, to allow us to traverse between several trees without hitting any. They loomed dark and foreboding. The car slid between, and I looked back to watch Fergus follow. *He couldn't have missed the trunks by much.*

We traveled slowly, the crunch of tires rolling over the native plants loud in the sudden silence before we veered back onto the road and waited for Fergus to catch up in his aged vehicle.

Now Christian used the accelerator, and we hurtled along the single lane road and into town.

At the one stop sign, we only just came to a halt before the car shot forward again.

There before us lay the Church. The small white building, older enough to remind me of my house.

We screamed to a stop outside the building. As we hurried for the door, it was as if an invisible barrier rose between us and where we needed to be.

Christian hammered at it, his hands glancing off, and I watched as fury suffused his face. Fergus had retrieved all manner of objects from his vehicle. The censer he swung sending out smoke while the professor anxiously checked every possible aspect of the building. We weren't getting inside until something happened. Something had to give.

A thought came to mind. "Christian?"

He stopped and looked at me, tears glistening in his eyes. "What?"

The thickness of his words was like being hit with an emotional avalanche. "I have an idea." Shaking started in my legs, but I'd do anything now for this man. For Kira. "I think... a sacrifice must be made," I said, unconsciously echoing the thoughts that slipped into my mind.

He blinked. "What?" His face paled.

I limped closer, my unstable ankle made it hard to maneuver, and it was as if my heart were being shredded because I knew exactly what I was saying. Suddenly there she was, Janet. In the flesh.

Except it wasn't a woman, so much as a creature. Her red-gold hair flying like whipping tails, her eyes glinting with red while welts scored her arms.

"You!" The word she spat at me, cutting.

I lurched in front of Christian. I would do this. It's what I knew had to be. "Let him in."

The woman growled, exposing long razor-sharp teeth. "No." She advanced, and I lunged, almost falling.

"Run!" I screamed, infusing the simple word with everything inside me.

"Tabitha!" I heard his bellow but was too busy watching her fingers fly at me, the nails sharp and black.

Had he left as I intended? I didn't know because my focus was on Janet. Or whatever she might really be. Her face contorted into a mask of hate and around me, waves of power surged.

I ducked, narrowly missing the sharp questing digits, but before I could rise, she was on me. Fingers digging deep. I yowled, but not before I heard the cadence, slow and methodical. *Fergus!*

Now Janet made to rise, and it was my turn to keep her still. Attempt to keep her grounded. I grasped her hands, screaming in pain, holding her tight with fingers that barely grasped her. The strength of the woman—demon—was astonishing. My fingers stung as she wrenched herself away and I glanced around, wind whipping my hair to and fro. A branch sailed through the air while trees bent and fought the onslaught of winds. I grabbed it and scurried behind her. Fergus stood, bible open in hand, and just as Janet made to attack, I hauled back. The connection of wood to skull echoed with a *thwack!*

Janet reared back as Fergus raised his voice one last time. She arched and screeched and we both took the opportunity to stumble and hop inside the church, my branch dragging along behind us.

The door closed and my chest heaved, pain alerting me to the many injuries I'd sustained as air settled into the puncture wounds.

My leg radiated pain that seemed to crawl through my leg and into my groin.

"Tabs!" Christian launched himself at me, and I oompah'd. "You're hurt. You shouldn't have—" He dragged me to a seat and settled me there.

"She had to. Tabitha knew exactly what she was doing." Fergus was riffling through a case and tugged out a vial. "We need to clean her wounds immediately. Otherwise it'll be too late." He moved with grace, unscrewing the lid and inserting an eye dropper. "You'll need to remove your jacket, dear."

I rolled my eyes but nonetheless did as instructed, though each move sent heat and pain through my body.

"Did she bite you, dear?" Fergus asked while the Professor watched on, eagerness filling his features. I looked at them both and had to wonder why they looked at me with such interest.

"What? No!" *Why would he ask that?*

"Demon bites are notorious." Fergus related. "Someone can be totally charming and good one day, then they get bitten and *poof*!" He made an action like an explosion with both hands. "Psychologists call it The Lucifer Effect. Me? I know it's the bite from a demon, but the world isn't ready for that disclosure. So instead, I keep track and visit those who've had a recorded change." He patted my arm and started applying small adhesive bandages to the areas he'd just doused.

I stared. Gob smacked at what he was saying, while the heat in every injury cooled and stopped the mad itching.

"She's going to be alright, won't she?" I heard the worry in Christian's voice and for a moment my vision clouded as anxiety spiked.

"Oh yes, but we need to hurry now. Show me the notes, the letters and the artefact." Fergus mumbled, putting the vial and dropper into a case. He tugged a small biohazard bag from his pocket and stashed the wrapping from the bandages in it.

"How did you get your bags in here?" I wondered aloud, and Fergus smiled.

"I only have two right now. The rest are in the car, but I doubt we'll need them immediately. These two contain my greatest weapons." He patted the bag as if they were old friends. I guess in his line of work they were, I thought, and couldn't contain the whoop of laughter.

All eyes settled on me and I pushed the laughter aside.

"Let's see the artefact," the priest encouraged.

Christian tugged it from his pocket and handed it to the Priest. Even from a distance, I felt the buzz it gave off.

Kira gulped audibly, and I looked at her. "I... *Let me have it,*" she growled, eyes taking on a red glow and her voice a deep and other-worldly register.

Peta half screamed and jumped, but Christian swooped down and grabbed his daughter. "Father?" Kira struggled in his grip, but he held tight, eyes narrowed with pain as he came face-to-face with her ancestry.

The priest sighed. "What is she, exactly?"

My hackles rose. "Kira's *not a creature.* She's Christian's daughter." There was a terse bite in my tones and the priest looked at me, frowned.

"I see. And is he...?" the Priest glanced to Christian.

Professor Leggett shook his head. "Her mother is part demon. You should bind the creature within the child, quickly. Otherwise..." He shrugged and looked regretfully at Christian. "She'll call the others."

I didn't like the words they spoke and tried to rush in front of the child, but the professor took my hand and drew me back. "He won't hurt her. Just stop the creature from creating more havoc. Then we can begin work on the artefact."

I waited as the priest grabbed a vial of water. "From the River Jordan," he informed us, then he took up his book and started chanting.

The surrounding air crackled and hummed. Powerful waves rippled in the air as he moved around the girl, spraying the water from the bottle.

Kira arched and screamed, her mouth foaming.

It terrified as much as broke my heart to hear the sounds and see the pain on Christian's face.

"I bind you, creature, and in the name of our Lord! I rebuke you..."

It felt like the ceremony took forever, as Kira jerked and screamed, eyes flashed red then back to her blue.

Finally, Christian was able to gather his daughter close. She was soaked with sweat, her long blonde hair sticking to her face and neck. The child sobbed into his shoulder and I watched, feeling helpless.

"You're done?" whispered Peta, and the priest nodded.

"I believe so."

"Then I can take her—"

Fergus shook his head. "No. We do not want those creatures outside to get near her. We may have rebuked and banished one of the creatures, but she'll be at risk until later on, when she's been baptized."

Christian stood, the child in his arms. "Then baptize her now."

"Time is of the essence right now. Let me see the artefact, then we can decide what should be done with it."

Christian's lip curled and he passed the wrapped package over, before retreating to the seats near the rear of the church.

*Should I join him? Would he welcome that or do I leave him alone with Kira for now?* Such indecision was removed from my hands when the Priest called me forward, shoving the package he'd briefly checked into my grasp. The buzz of connection felt stronger, more terrifying because of this.

Fergus pinned me with a long stare. "You're from the Captain's line, I believe?"

"I... Yes." I nodded.

"I hope there were no cuckolds in your line. That will make this safe, though the Professor is sure, given the dreams you seem to be having. Come here and assist with opening the package. But first, we take a prick of blood, coat your fingers. Necessary," he explained, "Because any protective charm must know it is of the same line to open it safely."

None of that made sense, but I let him nick my finger and draw a few drops of blood, which he smeared over palms and fingertips. He then held my hand over the oilcloth, so a tiny bead dribbled onto the material. The whole time I couldn't help but gaze at Christian. His face furrowed with concern as he held Kira to his chest.

A loud crack echoed, and I looked up to the windows to see a massive limb from one of the trees swaying madly, the breeze rising to a wild storm.

"What's going on?" demanded Peta, who advanced toward me.

"They are gathering their forces to retaliate. They want whatever we have here. Badly enough that they'll attempt to enter holy ground," Fergus answered. "Professor, in your readings, have you seen such as this before?"

There was a gaiety to the question, and I wondered at it.

"I have. But only when it's a secondary relic." The professor frowned. "Is that what you think this contains?"

"I do," answered the priest.

"What's a secondary relic?" I asked, my hands shaking.

Fergus sighed. "I'll explain later, but for now, I need to unwind the cloth surrounding the item."

With care, I touched the edge of the material and slid one finger beneath it.

*Suddenly I was thrust into the darkness, where Alice and the Captain waited. Side by side, yet it was as if neither could see nor sense the other.*

*"You have come so far, Tabitha. You must finish this. Help me to find my love so we can escape the endless torment of this place." Her face was pale, the gown tattered, and for the first time I felt the fear of the ghostly woman before me.*

*"You must finish this task, Tabitha. Without it, no one will be free. Not your Christian or his daughter. See how she shakes?" As if a portal opened, I could see the shivers wracking Kira's frame.*

*"But she's innocent, and so am I."*

*"Yes. You are also tasked with finishing my mission. Out there are demons who would use this item. You know and can feel it. Do not let them win, child. Everything depends on you now. You alone."*

Suddenly I was back, the chill of the church invading my bones and Christian's arms around me.

I turned, aware I lay on the floor, the parcel still in my hands. "What happened?"

"You fainted, Tabs." He held me tight and I soaked up the heat from his body.

"I didn't faint."

His mouth had taken on a grim thinning. "You frightened me, and Kira."

The little girl was crouched beside him and I reached out, touched her face. "Are you okay, Kira?"

The little girl sniffled and nodded.

Fergus and Professor Leggett watched in silence while Peta prowled by the door.

I struggled to stand. "This is getting seriously inconvenient," I muttered. "They told me it's my task. I must finish it." Now when I looked to Christian, there was determination but also a hint of terror.

"Alone?"

I nodded. "That's what they said."

"Who were they, Tabitha?" The professor touched my shoulder and I jumped.

"The Captain and Alice. I saw them both, but they can't see each other. It's like they're in other places at the same time. They can see me, but not each other."

"We must open the package, Leggett," growled Fergus.

Christian took my hand and led me to a chair. I settled down with the package on my lap. As I slid my finger under the wrap, the wild crescendo of wind rose, battering at the glass.

"You must hurry, child," urged Fergus, and I slipped the oilcloth from the box. My hands shook so hard I could hardly hold the wooden container. I reached for the lid and it was like everyone within the tiny building held their breath.

Another layer of wrapping, but this one was wet. I raised my eyes. "It's damp." I whispered.

Fergus and the Professor exchanged glances.

I made to lift the lid.

"Just a moment," called the professor as he hurried back to his suitcase and pulled out the tiny bottle of holy water once more. He squirted me and my hands with it, and I glanced at him in surprise.

"What was that for?"

"Think of it as insurance," muttered the priest.

I opened the wrapping and there lay a sliver of bone. I looked up at the priest. "I have no idea what this is." I passed the box to him and as I did a piece of parchment dropped from the bottom of the box.

*Bone of the Saint Agnes of Rome.*

"I've never heard of her. Have you?" I turned to Fergus and he nodded.

"Indeed. She was beheaded by the son of a Prefect of Rome who wished to marry her. I don't understand why this would be important though."

Professor Leggett muttered and had his head down, fiddling with his phone. "Give me a moment and I'll see if I can find out who..."

Kira, meanwhile, paled. "That's someone's bone? Are they dead? Like, ewww!"

Christian stared at her. "All for this?"

Fergus cleared his throat. "Depending on what Leggett finds, there's likely a good explanation as to why they want it." He waved in the direction of the door.

Leggett sat up. "Yes, of course. I knew I'd seen it somewhere. There was a story, stating that though the child was killed as an innocent in Rome after she'd pledged herself to the Holy Father, he wasn't quite what he seemed. The son involved; I mean. There were suggestions he was odd. Cruel and participated in unspeakable acts."

Fergus' eyes narrowed. "Involved in dark crafts? That would fit. They wanted the girl, a pious virgin who'd sacrificed herself for the church, protecting the innocence. They will always try to take control of such because they beget stronger demons by breaking the faith of those they impregnate."

"Okay, but what on earth does that mean for me, this artefact and why Michael and Alice are stuck in purgatory?" My lips felt stiff.

"My dear, it's actually quite simple," answered Leggett. "He was delivering this to the cathedral in Toowoomba. St Patrick's I believe. It was to be part of the altar. That's where they interred such items, during the consecration, according to what I know."

Fergus nodded in absent agreement.

"So, what do we do now?" Peta's voice echoed in the church. "Because they're going to try to get in and will likely succeed. Like, soon!" Peta was right, as the walls and roof rattled, wind blowing in savage gusts while the glass shuddered.

Leggett's fingers flew. "Fergus, you need to get on the line to the cathedral. We're going to have to get it to Brisbane and quickly."

A light glowed, gaining strength in the center of the nave. A face and form appeared before me.

I knew the dark blue coat and the shiny gold buttons. It was the Captain.

The others gasped as he became almost corporeal. "You have done very well, Tabitha. But there is one last task to accomplish, that will release me. You must deliver the relic to the Bishop. I have no doubt the priest here will assist you. Christian, you must accompany her. Ensure her safety, then find Alice's final resting place. Only then will we be together once more. For eternity. I will remain with you, child. But the last hurdles will be dangerous."

He turned now, to look at Peta. "You will protect the child, won't you, Peta?"

She gaped. "You know who I am?"

His smile was kind. "I know those who came from what I was. The child, Kira. She was meant to be, and in time, she too will face her own challenges. But for now, she is free of the taint, thanks to the efforts of this priest."

When he turned back, I had the impression he was bidding me farewell, if not for the last time, then for a long while. Tears pricked my eyes. "Farewell Tabitha. God speed."

Then his form wavered and winked out. The light disappearing.

"Leggett. You stay. I'll take these two and the relic with me to Brisbane. When is the next ferry Christian?"

Christian gaped at the priest, "Uh..."

"Later this morning," I answered, understanding that the situation the Captain had thrust upon us meant leaving his daughter behind.

"I can get you to the mainland faster," offered Peta, but Fergus shook his head.

"No. You must stay with Kira. Leggett will follow behind. I need my car. It's been... modified, if you will, for these circumstances."

I gaped at Fergus. "Modified?"

He shrugged. "When one is in my line of work, it becomes a necessity otherwise I would be inconvenienced by demons, rogue ghosts and the suchlike."

*Suchlike.* My mind whirled at what else there might be out there leading to such modifications being required, but didn't argue. I'd just been instructed by a ghost to take a bone from a long lost—and unknown to me—Saint to the cathedral in Brisbane for dealing with by the Bishop.

Under instruction from Fergus, who claimed he shouldn't touch the shard, I wrapped everything back up, and rubbed my blood over the cloth. He spoke in low urgent terms I couldn't understand, but heat suffused me.

A flash of light briefly illuminated the church, then Fergus returned to his bag, hunting through it until he withdrew a necklace and a long metal sword.

"You wear this amulet, Tabitha. It won't fully protect you, but all we need to do is get to the car. And Christian, this is for you. It was created in the Holy See, each time it was cooled, it was in water containing blessed water, and within the center of the sword is metal from various holy relics. It will let you destroy those who come too close to Tabitha. Above all, do not let them take that box from your hands, Tabitha."

Now he donned vestments, kissing the end of the stole he placed over his shoulders and raising the bottle of holy water and his bible in the other hand. "Fergus, pack my things up and hold on to them. I'll be in touch."

We formed a line, Fergus at the front, Christian at my back and I clutched the package with trembling hands. Out there, I heard wild snaps and howls.

"They'll come at you in many forms. Stay with us, do not get separated and we will keep you safe." In Fergus' voice I heard steely determination and nodded.

He cracked the door open, and slowly, murmuring prayers, we left the safety of the tiny church.

## CHAPTER 22

error filled my veins. Every step some creature, large or small, but all black with red eyes and slavering mouths came at me.

They clawed at my clothes before retreating with yowls.

One managed to reach with long, tentacle like fingers, winding around my legs as rain began to fall. It released me, cursing in a language I didn't know, eyes slitting into hate filled orbs.

A deluge out of season while the wind continued its raucous wail. A creature pulled at me and I slid. I kicked out and nearly fell, but Christian was there, sliding his hand around my wrist while wildly swinging the sword.

It connected with a creature who screeched and screamed. It felt like there was a bubble I had to push through, but I couldn't quite penetrate its skin. Every step harder to achieve than the last, although we were only meters from the car.

Creatures danced around us. Taunting and jeering.

And where we needed to go, there stood Janet, sneering at us.

*The woman who'd been married to Christian.*

*The mother of his child.*

Her true form was ghastly. Black scaly skin, red eyes and gnashing teeth and feet elongated, ending in claws.

"You won't escape me, Christian. I waited far too long for that."
She extended a long razor-sharp nail in the direction of the box I
carried. "Put up with everything, from a squalling brat to your
grasping sexual exploits that couldn't even satisfy a stick." Revulsion
dripped from every word. "But tonight, we will take the shard and we
will be victorious."

My breath escaped in pants, every exhalation blowing a white
cloud in the suddenly frigid chill. What she said... We couldn't let
them win, because suddenly it occurred to me it wasn't just Michael
and Alice's soul on the line. It would be countless souls. How many
other times had this skirmish taken place before? I'd known this was
an important battle, but now the gravity of the situation impinged
on me.

"Leave him alone," I growled. The horror of everything she said
pushed buttons deep inside me. The ones that felt this urgency to
stop her, whatever the cost.

"You will die. Just like *he* did. Painfully and alone." A voice echoed
through the night. Dark and frigid. It chilled me to my core, and I
turned.

Here was a beast of nightmares. It walked on two legs, like a man.
The vague outline of one was there, but that's where the similarities
came to an end. A long tail, horns and skin like ebony shone in the
weak sunlight.

"Hand me the package," the creature before me demanded,
extending its hand.

"No." I stepped closer to the priest who bellowed as he was
propelled back, and then there was a loud crash somewhere
behind me.

The creature whipped his hand out and flung Christian aside as if
he were a mere inconsequence. I heard a crash, my heart constricting
at his groan of pain. Tears stung my eyes and I blinked them away.

"Tabitha, you cannot give in," Fergus called out.

My belly shook, and my mouth dried. I licked my lips, because
now it was me. Just me alone, who could get to the car.

Janet screamed and flew at me. *Flew!* Nails extended, and I crouched as she neared. The fetid wind of her breath fanned over me, but she sailed past, hitting the side of the building with a crunch.

I didn't dare look to see where Christian and Fergus were. I had a feeling if I turned my back, this would all be over.

Rising, I stepped closer to the car and something else rushed me.

As if it were transferred to my brain, a prayer began escaping my lips. "O Divine Eternal Father, in union with your Divine Son and the Holy Spirit..."

"You cannot defeat me. Give me what I demand."

I kept my eyes on the car, because that's where I needed to be. Fergus had said it was modified. I gulped, because everything hung on me getting there. "...Heavenly Father, give us the reign of the Sacred Heart of Jesus and the Immaculate Heart of Mary. I repeat this prayer out of pure love for You with every beat of my heart and with every breath I take."

Now things started flying. Rocks, shrubs and leaves quivered and sailed through the air. The demon who demanding my obedience stalked toward me. I moved faster, more than a little aware that I wasn't fast enough.

I'd reached the door when something latched onto me. Hard. Nails digging deep, piercing skin and I screamed, even though I kept clutching the package. "You'll have to kill me to get this off me!"

A snarling laugh cracked through the air. "Very well." The scent of Sulphur made me gag. "If that's what it takes." Amusement laced the words, and I closed my eyes, once more recounting the prayer foremost in my mind.

A wild cacophony started. Sounds. Voices and I cracked my eyes. Christian had risen, crawling toward me, his face bone white and streaked with blood. He dragged the priest who groaned even as he clutched his tools to his chest.

I turned back. Ready to face oblivion.

Wisps of vapor started to appear before my gaze.

Ghosts. Hundreds of them. Men and women, some who looked a lot like me. Michael and one other, similar of face and shape.

They formed around our battered group.

I saw my father among them. "Daddy?"

He smiled. "I'm here, Tabs. You've done well, but now we are free to help... a little. Make for the car while we hold him off."

"Christian? Can you see this?"

He nodded. "But as they said, we need to move. I'm not sure Fergus will make it through another attack."

Nor Christian. His arm bent at an odd angle and the way he clutched at his ribs with the other arm, though he kept a tight hold on the sword, having dropped his grip on Fergus.

"Where are the keys?" I demanded of Fergus.

"Ig-nition."

I rose and tugged on the door. It opened, and I turned back, eyes taking in the wild melee for a moment. Ghosts insubstantial sliding around and through the demons that tried to engage them. Time was short, but I needed Fergus in the car and Christian too.

"Help me get him in the car," I muttered, sliding one hand under Fergus's jacket and finding his armpit.

Christian rose, a hiss escaping his lips.

He threw the sword to the backseat and we tugged and pulled, getting Fergus settled.

Christian climbed in with the older man and I slid inside as the Demon's eyes connected with him. His claws sliding through and extinguishing a ghost as he started running toward me, fury lighting his face.

I dragged the door shut and felt the thud and shudder of the car as the creature hit it.

Starting the car as it rocked, I squeaked and cried and prayed for help, fingers fumbling on the key. It started and Fergus spoke, the sound wet. "Get the radio on and turn it up," I looked into the rear mirror and saw the determination there. Followed his instructions and started, realizing it was a hymn. I turned the dial, raising the volume, and the creature bellowed.

I saw it through the windscreen.

"Now drive, Tabitha. As if our very lives depend on it. Which they probably do."

I slid the car into drive, slammed off the brake and accelerated.

The demon held still until the last second, jumping out of the way.

"Head for the ferry," demanded Fergus and I drove back the way we'd come. Slewing through the underbrush, the entire time aware of the sound of wings flying above us.

"He can't touch us in here, can he?"

Fergus smiled. "No."

In the back of my mind came the concern, 'what about on the ferry?' I kept that thought locked up. We'd no doubt cross that bridge as we got to it.

We barreled down to the wharf and thankfully they were already loading. Fergus called to Christian to drop the window and spoke with the sailor. He looked at the battered man on the back seat, accepted the payment and instructed us to drive on.

The car was fastened to the ferry with tight chains, and my gorge rose. "What about when we're at sea?"

Fergus pinned me with a tight gaze.

"When I boarded, I blessed the craft. Unless there's more than one ship, we're safe. For now."

The words didn't fill me with confidence, but it was as good as we were going to get. I huddled down in the seat. We'd elected to stay in the car for the hour-long crossing.

"Christian, how badly hurt are you?"

He shook his head, face tight. "My arm is broken, and I think a rib or two."

"We need to splint it," I said and started to turn, wondering if I should crawl over the back and render medical assistance. Not that I was ever really good at that.

"First aid kit. Under the passenger seat," groaned Fergus, his voice weaker than before.

"We need to get you to a hospital," Christian muttered.

Both of them, I thought.

"We need to get to the Cathedral. The bishop will be waiting for us," Fergus groaned.

Guilt flooded me. I was at least reasonably untouched, but both the men in the car were battered and in need of medical assistance. But I also understood the importance of getting to our location swiftly. My gaze settled on the oilskin wrapped box on the seat beside me. So much damage and loss for something so little.

Mental calculations rattled in my brain. Two hours, give or take should get us to the cathedral. Christian would be hurt, but safe enough. I wasn't so sure about Fergus.

The crossing was rough, water spraying the sides of the ferry. Washing over the deck and more than once I wondered if the demon was responsible for the rough conditions. It made sense if they were. That notion raced around my psyche, reinforcing my fears so they grew and took on a life of their own.

The ferry lurched and groaned, the trip feeling endless and my stomach pitching along with the waves.

Unsecured items flew down the deck and more than once I closed my eyes, sure we'd sink.

The ferry docked, sailors shaking their heads, and finally we disembarked.

The car jerked forward onto the dock.

A crack sounded.

The boat jerked.

Something flew past us as I slewed the car onto the asphalt.

Screams. People running.

Looking back, I saw the damage the thick cable had wrought. A large jagged tear in the hull while above us lightning cracked. Purple-red.

"We have to get on the road," I called, pressing the horn to encourage the car ahead of us to move

I pulled onto the road and floored the accelerator. "I hope this can go fast," I muttered. "Get your Bishop on the line, Fergus. We're going to need help."

The skies clouded over, and the rain descended. Heavier than the chunks of hail. They hammered the car, pelted the glass. Each time they connected I jerked, sure the projectile would crash into the vehicle and we'd die.

We couldn't afford to stop, so I swerved, lights cutting through the gloom as I hunched over the wheel. More than once I came too close to a vehicle ahead of me, the darkness and rain obscuring my view.

The car aqua-planed, and I slid my foot off the pedal, letting it slow naturally, the admonishments of my father about breaking a continuous loop in my head. Pounding started in my head, pulsing behind my eye as the mother of all headaches loomed. I willed it away. Not that the strategy worked.

The city loomed now, a beacon ahead, and I watched the fuel indicator, which was sliding too close to empty for my liking.

A tree shivered as we passed it. I was sure I saw leathery wings.

I shook, the temperature plummeting further, the blacktop of the road wavering, all the while dimly aware Fergus was on the phone, explaining what had happened.

"Slow down," urged the priest, and I did as we entered the outskirts of the city. "Take the next left, then the first right." I did as he instructed, not knowing my way around.

"How much further," gritted Christian.

"End of the road. A door will be opened. Drive in." Fergus answered.

I followed the instructions and drove inside.

"Turn off the engine," he said.

I did.

A door opened, and in walked a man, wearing elaborate robes. He reached for the rear door. "Well Fergus, it's a fine mess you've brought here today."

Fergus coughed, and bright red stained his lips. I started to scurry from the seat as the man turned and called for assistance.

Christian struggled forward and limped toward me. Once more I scooped up the package, but my free hand burrowed into Christian's.

"We made it. And we're alive."

"Yes, you did well. Bring the item with you." He turned, and we followed. The echo of our footsteps the only sound as Fergus was left at the vehicle attended by med-techs, I guessed.

We entered a large nave; the length filled with pews.

At the end, we stopped by the alter. "The package please, dear."

My gut quaked, but I handed the package over. The man unwrapped it as priests entered, followed by nuns in black and white habits.

One came close. "Come. You'll want to rest and your man here needs attention." She took my hand in hers and lead us to a side door.

# CHAPTER 23

*I*t was amazing, watching on the video feed. They took the piece of bone, treating it with such reverence and opened a box on the altar. Placed it inside.

Tears slid down my face, knowing that finally, we'd been able to fulfill Michael's task. Not that we'd got it to Toowoomba. The piece would become part of the greater Cathedral collection. "We have an extensive reliquary collection here, my dear." The nun informed me, plying me with hot sweet tea while the doctor was busy with Christian.

Fergus's injuries required him to be admitted to the hospital run by the church, but I'd been informed he'd make a full recovery.

"I know you have questions. The Bishop will be along shortly to answer what he can, but I must be excused. I have prayers before I meet with our potential postulants."

She left the room on silent feet and I waited in the room I'd been shown, feet tapping because there was a sudden sense of aloneness I was wholly unprepared for.

The door opened and the man who'd met us downstairs entered the room. "My dear, you will have many questions and I will answer what I can." He took the seat the nun had vacated, poured himself a tea and selected a coated biscuit, with, "I do wish they wouldn't put these chocolate ones out. They're not what my doctor allows." He took a bite and smiled at me.

"Not many questions, Your... uh, Priestliness?"

He laughed. "Usually I'm 'Your Grace', but just call me Frederick. I prefer that, my dear. You did well. It must have been scary."

Memories of the ordeal circled in my brain. "Tell me why one man was chosen to bring it here, and why was it so important that he died?"

He sighed. "It's hard to know. The artefact or relic was a second tier, meaning the person who it came from was in the presence of Jesus, Mary or an apostle... someone of that stature." He scratched his head. "Why one man? I doubt we'll ever know. I can guess because he was devout, or had worked for us before. We'd had dealings with the Queen, as far as I've been able to glean over the years. Reliquary such as this should never be treated lightly." He looked at me with what I'd describe as a million-mile-stare. "Sometimes they're called to it. Sometimes the church demands it."

His answer freaked me out a little bit. Especially the stare.

The door opened and Christian limped in. His face still pale, and I noted the slight dilation of his pupils.

The man assisting him steered him to a seat and settled him.

Christian reached out and took my hand in his and I turned back to the Bishop.

"So, Michael and Alice? Will they... you know, go on to heaven?" An inane question perhaps, but he smiled.

"I had the records from the church at the time retrieved from the archives. Fergus told us the Captain's request. I've the location of the burial site. She's on the location of the cottage, and as I happen to know people who know people, made the odd call." He smiled, satisfied if the twinkle in his eyes were anything to go by. "The resumption of the cottage is to be halted immediately. There can't be any kind of development. I can't totally stop the wheels of government, but the site will be protected now as a burial site."

My breath caught. She'd been nearby the whole time?

"And my eviction?"

His face turned sad. "I can't interfere in that. But you will be fairly recompensed, my child."

Shock rippled. I'd still have to leave, after all this. "But…"

He held up a hand. "It's not right, I understand your sense of loss and devastation, Tabitha. There have been generations of your family raised there. I would do more if I could, but the separation of powers precludes my further interference in the matter."

I rose, releasing Christian's grip, and strode toward the window, glancing out. The dark clouds that had covered the sky were retreating. "What do I do now?"

"You take this man home. You nurse him back to health and we'll be in touch." It felt like a dismissal and I turned, mouth open, ready to argue.

He shook his head. "It's not been in vain, Tabitha and Christian. Go home for now. Rest. You will be safe because you've completed your task." Then the Bishop withdrew.

## EPILOGUE

*S*itting at the table, I looked out over the night sky. Since the mad flight to the Cathedral three weeks ago, life has been quiet. Christian insisted I should stay with him. At first it was awkward, realizing that Kira knew I shared a bed with her father.

We emptied the cottage, and I cried this morning when we handed my keys over to the government official. Before we'd left, I walked to the location of Alice's grave. It was hidden by a rise, a small marker the only sign that she'd been buried here. I'd also received a letter from the Bishop, detailing Michael's resting place. In London.

I hunched down and laid the small posy of flowers on her grave. "I freed him, Alice. I hope he can free you too."

It didn't really seem enough, but it's all I had. Christian slid his arm around my waist. I settled back against him, gazing out to sea, wondering what would happen next.

Now, as I think back, I wonder if the seed that's entered my mind is accurate.

I reach into my bag and retrieve the small box, biting my lip. Three weeks had passed and though we'd returned here, nothing concrete about my arrangement with Christian was solidified. I thrust the box back, too chicken to follow through.

He entered the room, plates in hand.

"Where's Kira?"

"She asked to spend the night with Peta. I thought it might be good. You and I have some things to talk about."

Now I bit my lip. *If only he knew.*

I rose, grabbed the wines he poured earlier and wondering if I should.

We settled at the table, and he took my hand. We'd taken to saying grace, so I dipped my head, ready to pray.

He let go of my hand, and though I frowned I waited.

Something unfamiliar slid into my palm and I raised my head.

Christian's face was pale and set and caught my gaze before I could glance down. "I need to ask you something, Tabs. It's important. Marry me."

My eyes dropped and I saw what he'd put in my hand. A small ring box. He opened the lid and inside lay a small golden ring, a single blazing ruby in the center of a ring of diamonds.

"I love you, Tabitha. I love your wit. I love your feistiness and I love your caring nature. When we were in the church, I saw how you protected Kira. I see the heart of you, pure and loving. I need to share the rest of my days and nights with you. Say yes."

My eyes watered and I nodded, overwhelmed with sensations of joy and completion. "Yes," I whispered.

With a shaking hand, he slid the ring onto my finger. "And we can always talk about children in the future."

I smiled, more than aware of the tiny box in my bag. I wouldn't say anything now. Later, well, we'd get to that.

Instead, I drew out a letter.

"Fergus wrote. He's on his way to Rome, they want details of the attack and he says it's not the kind of thing you send in a letter." We both laughed, then I grew pensive. "I just wish I knew about the Captain and Alice."

As if I'd flicked some switch, the room dimmed, and I gripped Christian's hand tightly.

*The Captain advanced. "You have done so well, Tabitha."*

*The woman who moved up beside him took the Captain's hand and I saw the radiance on her features. "Thank you. I'm found. The Captain and I are free. Before we leave, we came to thank you. Both of you."*

*Tears dribbled down my cheek. "You've found each other. I'm so glad."*

*Alice reached out, and I felt the caress of her hand like a warm breeze on my skin. "It needed both of you for our mission to succeed and to bring us together once more. No longer are we afraid to go beyond. It's time."*

A flash of light blinded me, and I looked away, shielding my gaze. As quickly as it came, it disappeared.

"We did it, Tabs."

I smiled at him. "We did."

"Kira will be disappointed," he said, and I laughed.

"She'll have other things to think on. Like helping organize a wedding."

A flash of concern filled me. "She'll be happy, won't she? I mean..."

Christian cupped my cheek. "After dinner, I have to ring her to tell her your answer."

That stopped me in my tracks. "She knew? You told her you were going to propose?"

His grin was broad. "She's better at keeping secrets than I thought. I took her shopping for the ring and she picked it. Said it felt like us."

My stomach lurched. It had been doing that a lot lately. I'd woken sick... My breasts hurt and while I was pretty slack at keeping track, I couldn't remember my last period.

What if..? If my hunch was correct... would I surprise them both? Tomorrow. After I took a test, that is. And if it's positive.

He leaned over and kissed me, softly. I returned the favor, then sat back in my seat.

I had a promise of eternity and love. What more could a girl ask for?

***Did you enjoy this book by Imogene Nix?***

*Feel free to leave a review on the site of your choice and keep reading to find lots of other books by this author!*

## INHERITANCE OF THE BLOOD BY IMOGENE NIX

*In the darkness evil waits...*

As a young bride Kira was whisked away from everything and everyone she knew, including her new husband and became Christina, an operative of the Displaced Persons Unit.

As the danger grows she sees an opportunity to save her husband Vasya and sister Serina. But nothing is the same. Serina is grown up —married and pregnant.

Vasya too is older and darkly forbidding. Trusting Christina doesn't come easily until a catastrophic event takes place. Now, knowing the truth everything he thought he knew is changed. But at a very high cost.

The four must work together to defeat the Demon, Zuor and the stakes are higher than they imagined and all could be lost.

---

*The burning at the back of her neck warned she was being watched. A quick glance didn't clarify it. Instead, she turned around in time to see her mother's face, pale. "Mama?"*

*She took a step forward, but her grandfather snatched her wrist.*

*The grip was painful, and Kira stilled. "Let your parents talk."*

*She didn't know what the topic of conversation was, but it couldn't be good.*

*The dappled sunlight seemed cooler than before.*

*Her father crooked his forefinger at her grandfather while they stood there. For a moment she wished Vasya had come with them, but he had to work. Just the thought of her new husband warmed Kira.*

*She only had a few minutes to contemplate her newly defined status as a married woman, when her grandfather pulled at her hand. "Come with me." He tugged and, confused, Kira allowed herself to be towed away.*

*A glance at her parents' faces stole any feeling of well-being.*

*"Grandfather?"*

*"Shh, my love. You must go." His grip was implacable and his face stern, but he shivered.*

*"What are you doing? Where are you taking me, Grandfather?"*

*They moved rapidly through the village they'd visited to sell their wares just that morning, and for the first time since they'd arrived in the market place she felt fear. What was wrong? Was it something to do with Vasya?*

*"You are in danger. We must send you away." The words confused her further. Send her away? Danger?*

*"Where is Vasya?" She stumbled over a stone, but he kept tugging her onwards.*

*With a quick glance around, he hauled her into a dirty laneway between the buildings. Kira gasped, trying to drag air into her starving lungs. "There's no time. We must get you away."*

*A nondescript shopfront lay ahead, and he pushed on the door. It rattled and opened with a loud groan. "Andre? Andre, are you here?"*

*An older man shuffled into the room, bent nearly double from the weight of the load on his back. "Marat? What do you want?"*

*"My granddaughter. They are coming for her and us. Get her away. Take her now, while you can."*

*The man's face clouded over. "Are you sure?"*

*"Grandfather, where is Vasya?" Fright had the blood in her veins pounding.*

*"Hush, my precious. Andre will see you well." He turned. "Whatever it takes, Andre. Take her now." With surprising speed, her grandfather whirled and was gone.*

*The man, Andre, eyed her. "Come this way, child. There is no time to be lost."*

*Eleven years later*

The tattoo of her heart and cry of terror woke her, as they usually did. Once again, as she had since that rapid flight from those who sought her, she found herself in a lonely bed. Hundreds of miles away from everything she'd dreamed of, in a house she'd built for them to share. As always, it left her wishing that Vasya had fled with her.

Instead, here she was, exiled without her husband. With a sob, she rolled over and let the tears fall.

Available from Beachwalk Press

**books2read.com/IOTB**

Direct Autographed Copy

http://bit.ly/2w6g4K6

cated, with the existence of Carstairs her could-be ex-husband and teenage daughter, Frannie.

In *Revenge on Cupid*, Diocail must take the ultimate chance and find his own happily ever after with Simone. Sometimes the past gets in the way and HEA's don't come cheap though.

———————————

The dusty, dingy little diner was full, even with its current state of cleanliness—or lack thereof. People from the surrounding offices didn't care about anything except the incredible, well-prepared food at a reasonable cost. They flooded in, like waves to the shore. As one tide left, another swept in.

"Honestly, Simone. I'm going to try getting his attention one more time. If that doesn't work, I'm out of there. I mean, how long can I keep trying?" Cara picked at the caramel tart she hadn't been able to resist with the cheap metal fork and flicked the blob of fresh cream that sat on top to the side of the plate.

"You've said that tons of times before. Besides, what are you going to do to get his attention? Hmm? Walk naked through the typing pool?" Simone bobbed the straw in her smoothie as she eyed her friend with a frown. "It's been what? Eighteen months since you saw him, and you've mooned over him from a distance ever since you met him. You need to move on, Cara. That is, unless there's something you haven't shared?"

The query was arch. Cara shivered even as she shook her head. "No."

Simone quirked an eyebrow, obviously unconvinced with the answer. Cara let out a deep sigh of frustration. "There's a position...it's only temporary, for a PA reporting directly to him." She speared a forkful of tart, chewed quickly and swallowed, before continuing. "In his office, full-time for the period of the engagement. I saw the memo yesterday. I mean, I have the skills, right? I can type, answer phones, make coffee, file, greet people. What's more, I can probably do it better than all those size eights in the typing pool that Ms. Jackman seems to prefer." She nodded thoughtfully. "All I have to do is get past the ogre in Human Resources."

Simone stared at her, disbelief clear on her face. "Girl, I so remember that woman. If you think you can get past her, you're doing better than I ever did. That's why I left Veha Industries, remember? Maybe it's time to haul out your resumé and consider some other options. Look for something better." Simone shook her head and billows of her crimson hair swirled through the still air.

Cara understood Simone only had her best interests at heart. But this time she knew the outcome would be different. Hell, she could feel it in the air. The tingle of expectation.

"Cara, the HR ogre will hang you out for breakfast before she offers you anything like a position in that office. Remember her mantra? Good looks and good work make for a positive workplace!"

Simone didn't sugar-coat anything. It was another great reason for their long- term friendship. Honesty. But Cara didn't want to hear the truth in the statement. Even if it was exactly as her friend said.

Cara nodded quickly. "Yeah, I know, but if I don't try, then I won't know how close I can get to him, right? And the only way to catch his attention is to get past *her* and see him in person." Cara quaked a little at the information she needed to share. The favor she needed to ask. "Anyway, I tidied up my resumé and dropped the application into a memo envelope yesterday, so it's too late to back out now. I mean, fortune favors the brave. Doesn't it? If I don't snag an interview, I'm going to visit the career advisor across the street and register with them." She shrugged. "I'll look for temp work until something more long-term shows up. I can see what they have on offer and well...who knows? Maybe a job with the right boss is just waiting for me. But I'd rather this worked out, to be honest." Her voice trailed off into a whisper. "I really wish he would notice me."

Simone took a long slurp of her banana drink, and Cara noticed her questioning gaze even as she squirmed. Finally, Simone nodded. "It's your funeral. So anyway, you'd better show me this memo if you want me to be a referee for you. I'm guessing that's what you need, right? I'll have to know what I'm supposed to say about you before they ring."

Cara smiled. "Thanks, Simone. I knew I could count on you." She slipped a piece of paper out of her handbag and handed it over. "Sorry it's a bit creased. It was in the bottom of my bag, I stashed it so none of the others from the pool would see. You know how it is."

Available from Love Books Publishing
**books2read.com/CelticCupid**

Direct Autographed Copy
http://bit.ly/2vs7wtS

# BIOCYBE BY IMOGENE NIX

*Can a cyber-enhanced warrior and a ship's captain find love together?*

Levia Endrado never wanted to be a warrior, but at seventeen she was deemed suitable for battle. After intense training and multiple enhancements, which gave her superior strength and healing ability, she was sent off to defeat the enemy—a killing machine with a mission.

When the war was over, she had to find a new life. At twenty-seven she's a washed-up veteran without a future. Or she was, until she met Sandon Daria.

Serving as a pilot aboard Sandon's spaceship the *Golden Echo* makes Levia long for a different and gentler life. But old hurts and even older enemies aren't so easily forgotten. Particularly when they come back for her.

Sandon is determined to show Levia that she's more than just a BioCybe...she's the woman who completes him. Getting close is just the first step, keeping her alive is an even bigger challenge, but one he's willing to take because the prize is their combined future.

---

Levia scanned the long line of other hopefuls entering the chamber. The large building in the center of town was cold, and she dragged her wrap around her body, even as she craned her head, looking to the high ceiling. She'd never before had an occasion to enter the testing complex, yet she'd seen the lines of teenagers every time they passed the building.

Once she'd asked her parents why the teens were lined up and her mother's face had shuttered. Her stepfather had just shaken his head and growled. They'd stopped her questions with a carefully uttered, "You'll know soon enough, Levia." The pain in her mother's eyes had been enough to shush her questions. For endless months afterward, her parents had traveled different routes to the educational facility she attended and Levia lost interest in the puzzle of that building.

Now, as she looked around, remembering that long ago spring day, it was her opportunity to find out. But she felt a surge of concern at what lay ahead. She likely wasn't the only one, given that there were probably two to three hundred seventeen-year-olds gathered in the one place. Ahead of her, she caught sight of a couple of girls, their arms linked together and wide smiles on their faces. Scanning the crowd, she became aware that, by far, a majority of those gathered displayed both fear and trepidation.

"All female subjects will enter through doors three, six, and seven. All male subjects will enter through gates four, eight, and ten." The speaker above her was loud, and she jumped before checking the numbers etched on the black metal sign over her head.

The massive doors beside her swung open, and now an uncertain silence reigned. Many of the youngsters hung back, clearly discomforted by whatever testing regime lay ahead. This was where they'd been told their futures would be determined.

"Oh gosh, I hope they only have an aptitude and psych eval. I don't think..." Levia turned to see the white face of the girl behind her. The girl had uttered what many must silently be thinking.

Levia dragged an unsteady breath in, her hand resting flat against the plane of her belly as she looked around. No one had entered yet. It was clear many were on the verge of taking the step, but still they hung back.

She straightened her shoulders. "I'm not afraid." It was always wiser to approach things head-on, she believed. When her biological father had died, she'd been one of the few to view his capsule before it was sent into the massive gray structure built to accommodate those who'd moved onto the next life realm.

Her legs shook as she wobbled toward the entrance. Beyond the doorway, she spied sealed cubicles and her heart stuttered. Why cubicles? Usually testing—med and psych—were in eval-units, hidden only by billowing white curtains. She glanced back, noting that others had taken the first step.

"Move along, subjects." Once again, the androgynous voice of the address system blared.

Of course, given it was her seventeenth anniversary of birth, she was technically considered an adult now.

She thought longingly of baby Rald and her half-sister, Elda, waiting at home for her to return, and the celebrations to be held that night. That made her smile. She would need to make them proud of her.

She entered a row and the tall Educational Specialist, the edu-specs as her peers laughingly called them, stopped her. "Present your credentials to the scanner."

She'd done this many times since the tiny implant had been slipped below the dermal layer of her skin at birth. The small unit in her wrist heated as her details were checked.

"Enter the first cubicle, Levia Endrado, and follow the instructions to complete your assessment."

Thus dismissed, Levia moved to the first unit, laid her palm against the scanner, and the door slid open soundlessly.

"Welcome, Levia Endrado. Take your place in the eval-unit." The soft contralto of the voice echoed after the door closed silently behind her.

"What are you evaluating?" Her voice was breathy, and she peered around.

"Your skills—physical and psychological. Your emotional and medical status. Your educational attainment levels."

It was an answer that shed little insight into the many things she was hungry to know. "Why do all seventeen year olds—"

"Take a seat, Levia. Then we may begin your testing."

If she'd expected an answer, she was sadly mistaken, she considered sourly. She dropped into the seat, the soft leather-like surface molding to her body.

"Levia Endrado, you are required to remove all non-specified apparel."

She jolted in the chair. "It's cold."

"The temperature will be amended. Remove the non-specified apparel."

Her misgivings grew as she dragged off the light wrap she'd brought with her, and then threw it to the floor at the side of the unit.

"We will begin, Levia Endrado. At any time, should you experience any malfunctions of the unit, simply depress the red button." It glowed and she grimaced.

Levia reclined against the chair and waited for the testing to begin.

The first examination was based on her understanding of the political system, where she saw herself, and her knowledge of the rights and responsibilities accorded through citizenship of both her planet and the commonwealth.

The second test was mathematical and scientific proficiency. It felt like hours had passed by the time she'd finished, and she lay limp on the seat, exhausted.

"Levia Endrado, you may rise. The sanitary unit will emerge once you trigger the yellow button at the door. Should you require refreshment, press the blue button and a restorative will be made available."

"Can I leave?"

"Negative, Levia Endrado. Your needs will be catered for in this capsule."

"Why?" Her voice hitched and true fear rose for the first time. Why did they keep her in the alcove?

"All will be revealed at the end of the testing cycle."

Levia looked at the now empty screen before hurling a curse word. It was met with silence.

The urgent throb of her bladder reminded her that she needed to use the facilities, so, with

a sigh, she rose and clambered from the seat. After attending to the needs of her body, she walked around the unit, peering at the door, but it was obviously programmed remotely. She poked and prodded, but it made no difference. With a huff, she headed back to the chair.

The moment she'd settled in, the viewing screen shone bright. "Welcome back, Levia. The next sequence will evaluate your psychological reflexes, then that will be followed up with the general knowledge portion of the evaluation."

"When can I leave?" It seemed better to ask bluntly, she told herself.

"Once the examination is completed. After the next set of evaluations, you will be subjected to the physical aspect."

"Then I can go home?"

"Levia Endrado, you will now complete the psychological test. This will be undertaken by one of the center's personal evaluators."

She frowned. Personal evaluators? She bit her lip, and the sting reminded her that this wasn't something to joke about. In her seventeen years, she'd only heard of personal evaluators being brought in once before, and that was when one of the girls at her academy had been in a serious accident. Both legs were amputated and her body's ability to keep her alive had been gravely compromised. Her peers had been informed that the girl had requested the assessment before she could request her support systems be disconnected.

"Levia Endrado, are you ready to recommence processing?" The emotionless voice echoed once more and she gulped.

"Yes."

Available from Beachwalk Press<br>
http://www.beachwalkpress.com

Direct Autographed Books<br>
http://bit.ly/BioCybe

# ALSO BY IMOGENE NIX

<u>Warriors of the Elector</u>

- Star of Ishtar
- Starline
- Starfire
- Star of the Fleet
- Starburst
- The Star of Eternity

The Star of Ishtar & Starline - Print

Starfire & Star of the Fleet - Print

Starburst & The Star of Eternity - Print

<u>Blood Secrets</u>

- The Blood Bride
- The Illuminated Witch
- The Sorcerer's Touch

<u>House Secrets (The Blood Secrets Continuation)</u>

- As Dawn Breaks (Coming in 2021)
- Immortal Consequences (Coming in 2021)

<u>The Automaton Series</u>

- Haven House
- Nobel Crest

**The Search Duology**

- Miss Elspeth's Desire
- Miss Isabelle's Craving

**Reunion Trilogy**

- War's End
- The Assassin
- Executing Justice

The Reunion Trilogy in Paperback

**Sex Love & Aliens**

- Tangled Webs
- False Webs (Sex Love & Aliens Vol 1)
- Covert Webs (Sex Love & Aliens Vol 2)

**21st Testing Protocol**

- Cyborg: Redux
- Children Of A Greater Evil
- When Evil Came To Stay (Not Yet Released)
- Finis: The War To End All Wars (Not Yet Released)

**Celtic Cupid Trilogy**

- Blame The Wine
- A Stranger's Embrace
- Revenge On Cupid

The Celtic Cupid Trilogy in Paperback

<u>Zombieology</u>

- The Reset (2018)— (Love At The End of The World)
- I Dream of Zombies
- The Six Million Dollar Zombie

<u>Knights of Pleasure</u>

- Silken Knights (Not Yet Released)

<u>Single Titles</u>

The Chocolate Affair (also in Print)

Falling In Love Again (Previously A Sapphire For Karina)

BioCybe (also in Print)

Hesparia's Tears (also in Print)

Tomorrow's Promise

A Bar In Paris (also in Print)

Inheritance Of The Blood (also in Print)

The Plan (also in print)

Loving Memories (also in Print)

Hero of Heartbreak Hill (also in Print)

My One & Only

Curse Bound (coming 2021)

Raspberry Dreams (Not Yet Released)

<u>Non Fiction</u>

Self Publishing: Absolute Beginners Guide (With Suzi Love)

<u>Written as Ciara Cave</u>

25 Curated Ways To Get Rid Of Telemarketers

Book Signings for Absolute Beginners

# ABOUT THE AUTHOR

Imogene is published in a range of romance genres including Paranormal, Science Fiction and Contemporary. She is mainly published in the UK and USA.

In 2010, Imogene Nix (the pen name not Imogene herself) was born. Imogene sat down and worked tirelessly for 3 months culminating in the book Starline, which became the first in a trilogy titled, "Warriors of the Elector." Since then she's had over 30 titles published and is now focusing on hybridising herself - with a mixture of traditionally published and self-published works.

In fact, she's taking control of many of her back catalogue books, which are slowly re-releasing as self-published titles.

Imogene is a member of a range of professional organisations world wide, and believes in the mantra of mentoring and paying it forward and is actively involved in mentorship (through NaNoWrimo and her vlog: In The Chair With Imogene Nix) and tutoring of new and upcoming authors.

In her spare time she loves to drink coffee, wine & eat chocolate and is parenting her spoiled dog and a ferocious cat along with her husband and 2 human daughters and looks forward to weekends away with her husband in their caravan "The Seven Year Hitch!" Do look forward to her caravan romance at some point!

*To Contact Imogene*

www.imogenenix.net
imogene@imogenenix.net

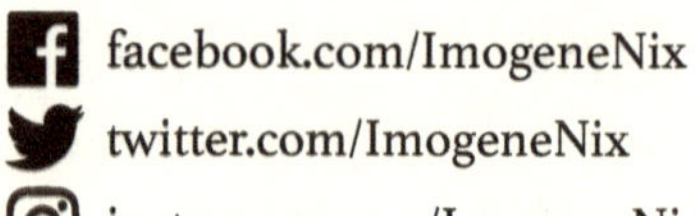

facebook.com/ImogeneNix
twitter.com/ImogeneNix
instagram.com/ImogeneNix